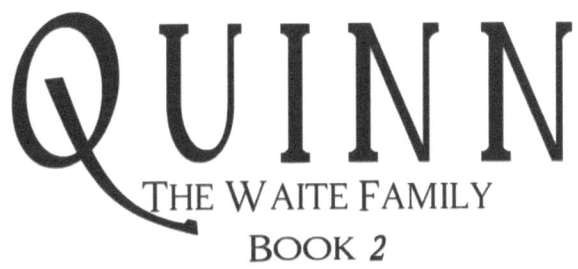

QUINN

THE WAITE FAMILY

BOOK *2*

KATHI S. BARTON

This is a work of fiction. Names, characters, places, and incidents are products of the author's imagination or are used fictitiously and are not to be construed as real. Any resemblance to actual events, locations, organizations, or person, living or dead, is entirely coincidental.

World Castle Publishing, LLC
Pensacola, Florida

Copyright © Kathi S. Barton
ISBN: 9781938243738
First Edition World Castle Publishing, LLC June 10, 2012
http://www.worldcastlepublishing.com

Licensing Notes

Cover: Karen Fuller
Photos: Shutterstock
Editor: Brieanna Robertson

CHAPTER 1

Drew listened to her. Well, sort of. He was hearing her speak, but he wasn't technically listening to her. Quinn Waite was the bossiest woman he'd ever met. Next to his boss, that is, who just happened to be her sister-in-law, Alyssa Waite. He'd leave her standing here, but he was serving food in the dinner line and couldn't escape just yet. But when he could, he was out of there.

"You have to make sure that she is safe, Mr. Miller. Here you go, Sally, have some extra potatoes. That woman said she'd get her back and we haven't...there's cream at the other end, Mr. Bane. Are you listening to me?"

"Yes. You want me to protect Alyssa who is probably more capable of protecting herself than I am, Sally has extra potatoes even though she didn't want them, and Mr. Bane now has a pocket full of creamers. Did I miss anything in your tirade?"

She glared and he laughed. It was either that or strangle her. Quinn was a woman who got things done, he'd give her that. But she wanted it done yesterday and damn the person who didn't pull their weight. Drew did pull his weight, but he did things in his own way on his own schedule. Not that he was lazy or a procrastinator, but he didn't feel that driving someone nuts to the point of wanting them to murder you was the way to go.

"I don't like you, Mr. Miller. Not one bit."

He grinned at her. "Well that's good, Miss Waite. I'd hate for all this hostility to be for nothing. Or even one-sided. Look, Alyssa is safe. She has a driver everywhere she goes and when she is at home your brother barely lets her out of his sight. At the office, you'd have to blow the entire building to get to her and—"

"Oh, Christ! You don't think someone will try that, do you? You have to put on extra people tonight. Better yet, I'll do it. And I'll hire some dogs. They can mill about the lobby sniffing everything that comes in." When she pulled out her little note book he snapped.

Taking it from her, he tore it in several pieces before he laid it on the counter and picked up the spoon for the mashed potatoes. Without breaking eye contact with her, he dumped the potatoes on the pieces of paper and threw the spoon in the sink. "I'm going home. You, Miss Waite, are certifiable. Mr. Bane, put the creamers back and go eat your dinner."

Drew sat in his truck and took several deep breaths before he started the engine. He didn't talk on his cell phone when he drove and he wouldn't drive angry. Laughing a little, he realized if he had to work the soup line with Quinn much more, he'd have to hire his own driver. Because the way he saw it, he'd never drive again.

Looking out the front window, he surveyed what he'd been able to be a part of in the past six months.

The Nathan Howard Diner was just one of many things that had been added to this very run down end of town. The diner would and did feed over two hundred meals a day, breakfast and dinner. There was enough food for anyone who wanted or needed it. So far, there had never been anyone turned down. Above the diner were rooms; big, fully finished rooms that ten men or women could sleep in and keep warm. There was also a small clinic, as well as a place for anyone to come and watch television and to read.

Just down the street, two buildings as a matter of fact, there was a library. Not the type run by the city or state, but one ran by people trying to establish a job history. Every few weeks or so, someone new would come in and be trained at one of the ten or so jobs offered. Then if they performed to some ability, Alyssa or one of her helpers, more homeless people, would work with them in some job in the company. From delivering mail to offices, running copies, or even just watering plants, anything and everything that required or didn't require a skill. It wasn't about the job; it was the dignity that came with having said, "I did this." So far they had been able to get seven people into some legitimate line of work.

The Rodney Kincaid Clinic was across the street from the Howard Building. It too was run mostly by some of the people trying to establish themselves back into the real world. There were doctors, of course. Alyssa's husband Cain was one of many that volunteered there several times a month. But there were also an amazing amount of people working there who either knew someone who still lived on the streets or sadly had disappeared on the streets, either by death or just missing. Hope was a very fragile thing and every one of them lived with the hope of helping someone who might be able to help their loved one.

Drew leaned his head back against the head rest and closed his eyes. He was working in the kitchen today because Alyssa and he had set up a schedule to have every employee who worked for Howard Enterprise work the kitchen. If anyone griped or ever tried to get out of working their turn they were fined, made to work a month straight at any capacity she needed them at. It had only happened once and that person was no longer with the company. Not that she fired him, no. Alyssa was too good of a person for that, but the person felt his views on what she was doing with her money were up for public debate. Alyssa was not doing this for some recognition; this was purely for her own peace of mind. Alyssa had spent ten years on the street recently to hide from her mother after her father died. It was a long and mostly terrifying battle, but she was back where she belonged at the helm of the richest company in the world.

When Drew had met her she had been looking for a hungry lawyer. His grandda had recommended him. Thomas Miller had worked for the Howard family for nearly five decades, serving first Alyssa's father, Nathan Howard, and now her. His grandda loved the younger Howard as much as he had the older, or so he'd told Drew just recently.

"She'll be making more money than her father ever dreamed of and she won't give a good hoot about it. You take care of my little girl for me, Drew. I can't be watching over her forever and I need to make sure that she is cared for."

"You sound as if you're planning on dying, old man. I won't have it, you know. You're all I have in the world and I can't…let's not talk about this again. I love you and the thought of losing you is just too much." Drew had his parents, and he loved them dearly, but his grandda…he was everything to him.

Drew was about steady enough to start home when a sudden rapping at his window startled him. Looking over without raising his head, he groaned. Damn it all to hell in a hand basket, wouldn't she ever give it up?

"I'd like a word with you please, Mr. Miller."

He nearly told Quinn to go away or better yet, just start his car and leave her, but it was impolite and he also didn't want to know what Cain would do to him if he found out that he'd left his sister in a parking lot alone. Not that he thought a mugger would stand a chance. She'd more than likely talk him to death.

He rolled down his window. It was still rude, but he wasn't in the mood to be that nice to her.

"I want to go home, Miss Waite. Can't this wait until in the morning? I'm tired and I just want to go to bed."

"I'll be quick." He nearly laughed, but could see she was serious. "I wanted to say that I'm sorry. I know that I can be a little overbearing—"

"A little? Try a lot. I know what I'm doing, Miss Waite. I've been a lawyer for a long time and I've not lost a client yet."

She growled at him. Actually growled. "I wasn't finished, thank you very much. As I was saying, I know that I can be a little overbearing at times, but Alyssa saved my life. I love her very much and worry about her. That being said, I think you could take my suggestions a little more serious in the future and let me have my way on some things."

Drew laughed. "That must have hurt a bit. I mean the hard-assed Quinn Waite saying she's sorry. Did you have to write it down and have it perfect before you came out here? Or did you just wing it? No, you wouldn't want to have anything to be wrong, would you?"

He saw the hurt in her eyes and felt badly for it. Before he could tell her he was sorry, there was a shout behind his truck and she turned away. When she smiled at someone and took off running Drew turned in his seat to see who it was. Another woman was getting out of a car and throwing her bag—was that a duffle bag?—on the ground. The two women embraced then walked to the Diner again. Drew started his truck and left the lot.

~~~

Quinn hugged Sin again. It was so unexpected to see her sister that she wanted to keep touching her to assure herself she was there. Sin, or Sydney as was her real name, was in the Army. A captain in the Special Forces, actually. They were on their way to Cain's house when Quinn asked her sister why she was home. Also, why she hadn't given them any notice that she was coming to visit.

"Don't. Just let me visit, okay? I'll only be here for a few days and I don't want to spend it trying to calm nerves and tell you I can't tell you. Suffice it to say I'm fine, my men are fine, and we are all hunky dory."

Quinn could tell something was off, but decided that trying to get anything from Sin if she didn't want to share would more than likely have her clam up like a safe. Quinn wanted to visit with her baby sister, not fight.

"I'm so glad you're here. You have to meet Alyssa. She's so cool and Cain is such a sap around her. He looks like one of those puppies in the window you want to take home. And her…wow, she's the same way. I was really glad when they let Jazzie and me stay in Cain's house and not with them. It's a big friggin' house, but still."

Sin laughed. It was a sad sort of one, but Quinn would take what she could get. Quinn was pulling into the deep drive when Sin asked a question that had her jerk the wheel.

"Who's the hunky guy in the truck that you were fighting with? He looked like he was ready to haul you inside with him or drive off without you. Something I should know about?" Sin wiggled her brows. "Have you finally met the right one?"

Quinn tried not to blush. She didn't want anyone to know what she thought about Andrew Miller. For one thing, he was way out of her league, and for another, she wasn't ever going to let herself think about ever getting herself tied up with a man again. Once was plenty.

Carl Wicket had been an abusive husband, both physically and mentally. She'd spent more than one night in the hospital and she wasn't going to put herself in that sort of situation again. Not that she thought Drew would hurt her, but she didn't want to hurt him. She was extremely gun-shy…or in this case, sex-shy.

Had it not been for Sin, Quinn didn't want to think about what would have happened to her if she hadn't learned to defend herself. When Sin had taken her to the gym and showed her how to fight back, it had been a rude awakening. Quinn hadn't even known that her family was aware of it.

Then when Carl had gotten out of the hospital after he'd been shot in the line of duty, he'd been his usual sweetness to her. About a week later when he drew back his fist to make a point she made hers first, knocking him down and hitting back. He'd hurt her, broken two ribs and bloodied her mouth, but she'd put him in intensive care for a week. He left her soon after and had signed the divorce papers and sent them back immediately. She'd not been out on a date since.

"His name is Andrew Miller, he's Alyssa's lawyer. He doesn't like me, not at all. Of course there isn't any love lost between us, but that's okay too. How about you? Dating anyone special?" She flushed when she realized how quickly she'd spoken. Apparently, so had Sin.

Sin's full-bodied laugh made people turn to look. She certainly lived up to her name—tall, muscled, and beautiful. Sexy.

"I don't have time to date. I'm with seven to ten men daily and not a one of them see me as anything but their captain. And I want to keep it that way. Being in the outer jungle and horny are not situations I ever want to be in." Sin turned in her seat to look at her fully. "But cute. Nice turn around. Answer the question, Quinn. What does he mean to you, if anything?"

What did he mean to her? Nothing. Not that she didn't want more, but he was pissed at her more than anything. She looked over at Sin and with the best straight face she could muster, answered her. "He hates me. Most of the time, I hate him too. He works for Alyssa and that's it, I swear."

Sin stared at her and after a few moments, she nodded then changed the subject. Quinn had never been so grateful to anyone in her life. She never thought talking about something so mundane as ordering bulk sheets and pillows could be so much fun.

CHAPTER 2

Alyssa and Cain were in the mansion when Quinn called. She told them she had a surprise and that she needed to bring it now. She told him she'd be over as soon as she took a shower and changed. Cain wanted to spend the night making love to his wife not talking with his sister, but Alyssa was right, they had become hermits.

When the butler opened the door an hour later Cain couldn't believe it. Sin Waite was standing on his doorstep. He didn't know how long he'd stood there before Gayle, the maid, poked him in the ribs to get him going again. He reached forward, pulled his sister into his arms, and swung her around the room in a great bear hug. "Damn it, woman, don't you ever call? I've missed you. You look great." She did too. But then Sin had a quality about her that made one see the entire picture rather than the big blue eyes and short dark hair. He pulled Quinn into a hug as well. He loved his sisters, all five of them, and was very happy to have them home with him, even if it was for a short time.

"Let me get Alyssa. She's in the study with Drew. They've been in there long enough." Cain turned and nearly bowled the two of them over in his haste. Picking up his wife, Cain hugged her too.

Drew stepped back with his hands up in the air. "You hug me like that and I'll knock you on your ass. It's bad enough that Grandda does it, I won't have—oof!"

Cain hugged him too. When Drew started to struggle, Cain pulled him tighter and patted the man on the back. He was just too happy to care what Drew thought. Smiling, Cain introduced them to his baby sister.

"Honey, Alyssa," Cain started with a grin and a wink to Drew. "This is Sydney Waite. Sin, this is my lovely wife, Alyssa Howard Waite, and her attorney and friend of the family, Andrew Miller. He works for Alyssa."

"He works for us both. Hello, Sin. I'm so happy to finally meet you. Cain and the others have told me all about you. Why don't we all go into the living room?"

Cain looked to the kitchen when someone cleared their throat. He didn't think he'd ever get used to having servants. And gardeners and pool people and…the list was nearly as endless as the things he'd had to do since marrying the richest woman in the world.

"Dr. Waite," the butler, Fredrick, asked him, "shall I serve cocktails and hors d'oeuvre? And would you like for me to set extra place settings for dinner?"

"If I asked you to set another place setting will there be enough for everyone to eat? Or do I need to have you order pizzas?" Cain was half kidding, but the man looked like he'd just stolen his last chocolate truffle.

He knew there would be enough food. For whatever reason there was always more food than they could eat at one meal. Cain had started taking the leftovers to work every day and feeding the staff and whoever else was hungry. But he always asked.

"Oh yes, sir, plenty. I shall have cook slow things down a bit then dinner can be served when you're ready. I'll just bring in something to hold you over."

Cain grinned. He'd introduced them to that term the first week here. Holding him over until his wife got home had become somewhat of a frustration to the people in the kitchen. Either have something ready for him or have the master of the house under foot in their domain until the mistress could lead him away.

"I know that Alyssa is hungry and even if she's not we'll eat in an hour. Thanks, Fredrick. And please see if Cook has anymore of that brown cheese that Alyssa likes, please?"

"Yes, sir, right away." Cain went into the living room just as Drew and Quinn were getting into another fight.

The two of them seemed to go at it all the time. Cain had noticed it just after the wedding. He didn't worry about Quinn getting hurt. For one thing, Quinn could handle herself and for another, Drew wasn't the type of man who would hurt a woman. But their constant bickering could grate on one's nerves. Alyssa said to let them go. She said things usually worked out better when there weren't too many fingers in the stew. He was sure she'd gotten that bit of wisdom from her friend Rodney.

"He didn't do anything but stand there and mash up potatoes on my note pad. All I was doing was making some notes. Notes, I might add, to ensure the safety of you, Alyssa." That got Cain's attention, but before he could comment or ask, Drew clarified.

"She was making notes on having dogs mill about the lobby of the Howard Building. Dogs! Do you…who was going to take them out to walk? Hummm, ever think of that? Or were you going to bring in trees and fire hydrants for them to use? Not to mention, can you imagine the look on the people's faces coming in for a visit to have dogs sniffing crotches? Holy Christ, don't you think things through?"

Quinn stood up and glared at Drew. "That's why I was writing it down, so I could think it through, you overgrown, narcissistic dick. I have never in all my—"

"I am not narcissistic," Drew said in a deceptively calm voice. "Nor am I overgrown. As for the 'dick' part…perhaps I could interest you in it sometime."

The sound of skin connecting to skin was profound. Cain could see both their faces and he didn't know which of them looked more shocked, Quinn or Drew. When blood welled on his lip Quinn stepped forward and Drew took a step back.

"Don't touch me." Drew turned to him and Alyssa and bowed. To Sin he saluted then he left the room. The sound of the front door closing was loud in the silent room. That was until Sin burst out laughing.

"Way to go, big sis. You just bloodied your opponent. I hope for your sake that he plays fair, because a man like him doesn't seem to forgive and forget."

Quinn left too. She simply grabbed up her purse and jacket and fled out the door and the driveway.

~~~

"Howard Corporation, Quinn Waite speaking."

Quinn had been at work for nearly two hours. She hadn't left her plush office nor had she gone to the meeting that was an hour ago. Her secretary had come in to remind her, but Quinn had begged off. She just couldn't face anyone after last night.

She still couldn't believe she'd hit Drew. She'd been mad, of course, but hitting someone was just...she didn't do things like that. She was becoming unhinged like her ex-husband. Then she realized the person on the phone was talking.

"I'm sorry, could you repeat that, please? I must have hit the volume button and didn't catch all that."

"I said that I'm looking to find someone to take my money. I have a bit of it and was wondering how one went about donating some of it to some of them causes that the Howard Foundation is working with."

Quinn got excited then froze. She didn't know why this person asking about the Howard Foundation made her nervous, but he did. All she could think about was the way Alyssa's mother and uncle had threatened to get Alyssa that morning.

It was an ongoing battle to have Alyssa's mother come into the building yelling and screaming. Shannon was what Quinn had always thought a harpy would be like. And also a woman who put her needs well above those of her children and anyone else. Alyssa simply hated her mother. Why she didn't ban her from coming in was beyond everyone who worked there. But Quinn understood. No matter what, she was still her mother. And a person just wanted their mother to love them. But the man on the phone was speaking again.

"May I have your name, please? I find I can work better when I have a—"

"I don't think you need my name to ask for information, do you, girly? I just want you to tell me how I go about donating money. Maybe you can tell me how to get in touch with Alyssa too." His voice had hardened and gotten meaner with each word.

Quinn looked up when her door opened. Drew stood there. She wasn't sure what he saw, but he was across the room in a second and standing next to her desk. He picked up her discarded pen and wrote her a note.

Tell me what they are saying.

Quinn shook her head and turned her back to him only to be jerked around in her chair and facing him. He pulled the phone slightly away from her ear and leaned close. She closed her eyes. Now how the hell did he expect her to concentrate?

"Are you there? Damn it. I want that information and you're going to…damn it, I lost the connection. What do I do now?"

There was mumbling in the background, but nothing she could understand. She watched Drew pull out his cell phone and start texting someone. She didn't care, not when he was this close to her. Trying to regain some control over the situation, Quinn rolled her chair back from him.

"I'm here. I don't understand what you would need to speak to Mrs…" At Drew's sharp look, she stopped.

"What do you need Alyssa for? I can handle any donations you want to give, Mr.….?"

The phone went dead. Quinn put the receiver back in its cradle and then looked at the man in front of her. He didn't say anything, but when her phone rang again, he snatched it up before the second ring. She stood up and went to the little bathroom just behind the desk and closed the door. She leaned back against the hard, cool wood and closed her eyes. Damn it, she didn't need this today. Or any other day for that matter.

She could hear Drew talking, not what he was saying, but the deep rumble of his voice as he spoke. Lifting the sleeve of her dress, she sniffed and could smell the expensive aftershave he wore. Lowering her arm, she walked over to the toilet and sat down hard on the lid. There was something profoundly wrong with her, she decided.

There was a possible threat to her sister and friend and she was in the bathroom mooning over a man who hated her. Okay, maybe hate was a strong word, she thought again, but he most assuredly didn't like her. She leaned back against the toilet and let out a sigh. She could be honest with herself here. She was nearly in love with the jerk. The tears welling in her eyes didn't do much to improve her mood about it either. When he knocked, she glared at the door.

"Busy in here. Go away." Her voice sounded watery and she hated that and cleared her throat to try again. But Drew spoke first.

"Get out here. I need to ask you what that person said. And I have a trace on your phone too, so don't be calling in porn call lines."

That had her up and jerking the door open before she could think. The nerve of the man. Porn lines indeed. She rounded on him the second the door cleared the jamb.

"You bastard. Get out of my office right fucking now. I've had more than…" She stopped when she realized what he was doing. "Why are you laughing? I don't find any of this…you know, I don't care. Get out before I call security, or better yet, Alyssa. She'll side with me." Quinn stomped her foot.

The second her foot touched the floor she knew she'd made a tactical error. It was the perfect girly thing to do and he'd witnessed it. Moving past him and toward the door, she was nearly out it when he grabbed her arm and turned her so that her back was against the wall. The door snapped shut.

"What did he…you've been crying. What did he say to you? Did he threaten you too? Damn it, Quinn, tell me."

He was close. Closer to her than he'd ever been, and she couldn't stand it anymore. She would blame it on the stress, she thought, and cupped the back of his head and pulled him to her mouth.

CHAPTER 3

Drew stiffened for all of a second then leaned his body into hers. Quinn felt good where she was, her body pressed under his. When her hand moved up to his hair and her fingers touched his scalp, Drew wrapped his arm around her shoulder, tilting her head with his chin, and his free hand pulled her hip closer to his. Need coiled in his gut and fought for freedom as their bodies lined up perfectly.

Drew felt her heavy sigh, the heat of her body, and the warmth of her mouth. All these sensations hit his system as she curled her fingers around his neck. He had a second to think about the woman touching him and then nothing, only the feel of her and her body.

Nipping at her lips, she opened for him and he slid his tongue inside of her. She tasted of the cherry turnover that was half eaten on her desk and sweet tea. She was warm and delicious at the same time, and soft and muscled beneath his hand. When he trailed his fingers along her ribs and cupped the weight of her breast in his palm, her

23

answering moan had him press his cock deeper into her softness, rocking against her over and over until he thought he would explode. Things went from the desire to touch her to needing to feel her body beneath his, her wrapped around him, silky sheets tangled about them.

He jerked back from her suddenly, wrenching his mouth and body from hers. He started to reach for her again when she stumbled, but drew back when she flinched from him. What the fuck was he doing?

She was panting and her eyes were dark with passion. Drew wanted to step forward again, only this time to take up where he'd stopped. But he couldn't, not with Quinn, not with the boss's sister. Not with someone he worked with, especially not one that he could barely stand most of the time. He watched her face, waiting for something, anything that would tell him she thought it was a mistake too.

Fire and anger blazed on her face to replace the dreamy look of unfulfilled passion and need. Had he not witnessed it, he would not have believed that a woman could go from one extreme to another so quickly. He started to tell her…he didn't know what he would say when she spoke first.

"Get out," she told him in a husky voice, whether from passion or anger he wasn't sure. "I want you to get out of my office right now." She moved toward the door again and opened it.

"I have to…you can't be pissed at me, Quinn. You kissed me first. A man does not, cannot pass up kissing a beautiful woman. I'm not—"

"My mistake. You can count on it never happening again. Think of it as a moment of stupidity. I want you to leave right now."

He didn't like that she sounded so…well, dejected came to mind, but he was more concerned by her thinking it would never happen again. And that brought him up short. It wouldn't, would it? No, of course not. He started toward the door and was nearly out it when he remembered what had brought him in here in the first place. He wanted to go to his office and think, to try and sort this out, but knew he couldn't. Not yet at any rate.

"You missed the meeting. There are things we need to go over and I have a list of things I need to make you aware of." He looked back at her desk. "Then we have to talk about that call you just received."

Quinn looked at her desk as if she'd never seen it before and Drew had a moment of panic. She wasn't all right and he knew it. This time when she spoke her voice was stronger and had a bit more bite in it. He was sure he liked it a lot better than the hurt one.

"I don't want to talk to you. Not now, maybe never again. Send one of your flunkies in or better yet, I'll go and talk to Alyssa. I should…I apologize for kissing you. As I said, it won't happen again."

Pushing the door at him, he could either leave with it closing or be hit by it. He was on the other side of it before he could manage to say anything else. He turned to look at the empty desk of her secretary and thought about waiting for her to come back. Knowing that he had to do something, Drew pulled out his phone and started for his office.

"Hello, May I speak to Doctor Waite, please? Tell him it's Andrew Miller and I just need a word with him.

~~~

Cain hung up the phone and sat back in his chair. Drew and Quinn had had a fight. Not that it was anything new, but this time, Cain knew it was different.

Cain knew that his sister had feelings for Drew Miller. But he didn't know how deep. And if he'd been asked, he would have said they were feelings of distaste. But he'd have been wrong. When Drew had told him that they had gone beyond mere workmates and he was sorry, Cain wondered for the first time what kind of feelings Drew had for Quinn. The man hadn't said what had happened, only that Quinn and he were having an issue, then he explained about the phone call.

That concerned him, but not as much as it did Drew. Cain knew that Alyssa had a constant guard on her at work and at home. The state of the art security system they'd had put in while on their honeymoon was manned twenty-four-seven. When she was at work, he also knew that getting into the Howard building was harder than getting into Fort Knox.

He grinned when he thought about her and him getting caught with their pants literally down when she screamed out her climax a couple of weeks ago. That had been both exciting and embarrassing. She still blushed when he came to see her.

He had dropped by to see if she could have lunch with him. She was sleeping in that oversized chair her father had left her. Her head was back on the rest, her feet up on the desk, and her skirt was just above those sexy thigh-highs she wore. Moving quietly to the side of the desk where she was he removed her heels and began to massage her feet.

Cain had never thought of himself as a foot man, but the sexily-painted toes of his wife made him dizzy with need. And the tiny gold chain that she wore around her trim ankle had his cock surge with aching arousal.

Running his hands up and down her calves then her thighs, Cain adjusted his cock in his trousers again. He finally pulled his belt open and unsnapped his fly. His cock strained to be free from the tight confines of his boxers. As soon as he touched her warm skin between the skirt and stockings he knew that he was going to take her on that big desk. Going to his knees, Cain ran his fingers under the hem of her skirt as he leaned in and nuzzled her breast. She moaned with him. He could feel her nipple harden under his mouth. Opening it just a bit, he took her nipple into his mouth and nipped.

"Cain?"

He looked up at her sleep filled eyes. "Who else, love, would be coming in here doing this to you?" Her grin had him nearly panting with need. "Put your legs over my shoulders, Alyssa. I need to taste your honey and cream."

Without hesitation, she lifted her right leg and draped it over his shoulder. Pulling her ass closer to the edge of the seat, he peeled her skirt higher up on her hips, exposing the dainty little panties and tops of the stockings to him.

"Alyssa, I'm going to lick you until you come then I'm going to pull you onto my cock and take you on this desk. My cock buried deep in this hot pussy over and over until I come too."

She wrapped her fingers in his hair and pulled him to her. Her scent, her need nearly had him come then. Her curls were wet with her need and he slid his finger deep into her as he watched her face.

"Please, Cain. I can't wait. I've thought about you all morning and I'm so ready to explode on your cock."

Cain leaned down and nipped the tiny bud of her femininity. She moaned and arched up against his mouth. Sliding in and out of her with his finger, he suckled at her pussy and drank from her. Her quick, hard climax had her tighten her thighs around his ears and fill his mouth with her. Over and over he licked and nipped at her, sliding in and out until he thought he would burst from it himself. When she came again then a third time, Cain used his free hand to pull his boxers down and stroke his cock. It wasn't enough, he needed more.

Still covered in her cream, he pulled her out of the chair and impaled her onto his cock as he came, roaring out her name as she screamed out his. When the door burst open as soon as they finished, he had scrambled to protect and hide her from the intrusion.

There stood her secretary, gun drawn and staring opened-mouthed at the two of them. As quickly as she came in, Rachel Dunning turned and left the room. Cain still got a chuckle out of it whenever he thought about it. She asked to be transferred to another department the next morning.

That was how Quinn had become Alyssa's secretary. It had been working out very well for the two of them, or so Cain thought. He knew that Alyssa seemed a lot more relaxed when she came home. And when she was at home, she was all there and her mind wasn't on what she had left at work.

Cain tried to remember if Alyssa had said anything about Drew and Quinn other than they fought a lot. Nothing. He leaned forward and dialed his wife. He might as well see what she knew. After explaining about what Drew had said he asked her what she thought.

"I think that whatever it is, we should leave it alone. If we try to step in, one or both of them will get pissed and I love them both too much to want either of them to be mad at me."

Cain agreed. "What do you think he meant by they had gone on to more than just workmates?" Cain wasn't sure he wanted to know, but knew he needed to ask. "You don't think they're sleeping together, do you?"

For whatever reason, Cain didn't want to think about his sister having sex. He shuddered when he thought about it. There were just so many things a man could know about his sisters. And their sex lives was way too much.

Her laughter brought him back to the present. "I think if she's having sex with Drew then he'd be a bit more relaxed all the time. I think if either of them were having the kind of sex we are and as often, they wouldn't be fighting so much."

Cain had to agree. Just the thought of being deep inside of Alyssa made his cock jerk in response. He started to ask her if she had an hour for him to come over and relax her a bit more when there was a knock at his door.

"I'm sorry Dr. Waite, but Todd Whip is here to see you. He said that it's important. He doesn't have an appointment, but I can squeeze him in now."

Cain nodded and waited for the door to close before he continued with Alyssa. Damn it, that boy was going to be trouble and he just knew it. Cain had a fleeting thought as to what he had been like at seventeen and shuddered. "I've got a patient. I was going to come over and see you. Maybe get in a little relaxation time myself, but duty calls. Will you be home on time tonight?"

"No. And neither will you. Remember? We have that dinner with your sisters tonight? We're meeting them at the Four Seasons. Don't be late, Cain, or I'll not show you the pretty little package I received today."

Her sexy laughter skimmed over his skin and heated his blood. Before he could ask anymore she hung up. He sat there holding the dead phone, thinking about her nude body on their new bed when a knock sounded again. He quickly hung up and adjusted his raging hard-on as he went to the door, thankful for the long lab coat. She was going to pay for that, he thought with a smile, just as soon as dinner was over.

CHAPTER 4

Cain was late. Alyssa was going to murder him if he wasn't already dead somewhere along the side of the road. She clicked off her phone again without leaving a message. The least he could do is answer his phone, she thought. Putting the phone into her pocket, she turned to her new family.

"He isn't answering. Let's go and sit and if he shows up we can all gang up on him and his lack of punctuality. I'm sure he's fine."

"And if he isn't," Sin said with a small smile, "he won't be when you're finished with him, correct? I like you, Alyssa. I think Cain will do well with you on his ass all the time. It's great to see that he's met his match in you."

Alyssa liked this sister, Sin. She actually liked them all. Sin was by and far the most outspoken, but Alyssa had been warned about that from Jazzie. She winked at Sin as they sat in their seats.

"I'm sure I have his number." The waiter left them their menus and took their drink order. "So when do you go back, Sin? I'm guessing you can't tell us where."

"No, I can't tell you where, but I go back tomorrow afternoon. This is just a short layover and I maneuvered it around so that I landed close enough this time to visit." She looked sad for just a second then brightened. "Seeing you all has made the hassle well worth it."

Sin had told them yesterday that she and her men were being shipped out again but didn't know when. Alyssa knew that Sin's commanding officer had called this morning and also knew that Sin wasn't happy about whatever he'd said to her. Alyssa smiled when she thought of the mouth on Sydney Waite and thought that she might have her teach her a few of those curse words. They were just ordering their dinner when Cain showed up.

Alyssa knew immediately that something had happened. When she started to ask him about it he shook his head and laced his fingers with hers and gave her a squeeze. She wanted to drag him to the nearest closet and make him tell her, but knew that he would do so in his own time. His sisters, if they noticed, said nothing to him about his mood. Dinner continued on and she was sorry to see that whatever was bothering him was affecting his time with his family. When they called it an evening, he pulled her into his arms in the parking lot after the women left.

"I'm sorry, baby. I just need you to hold me for a minute. Then I'll tell you, I promise."

Alyssa held him; she would hold him forever if he needed it. "You're scaring me, Cain. What is it? Your mother? My mother? Oh God, she's starting on you again, isn't she. You can tell her for me that no matter what she tries, she is not getting—"

His kiss cut her off. It was hard and slightly painful at first, hot and unforgiving. Then it changed. It changed into more. More heat, more mouth, and more touching. When a horn blared behind them, Cain broke it off, but didn't step away from her. He leaned his forehead against hers.

"We need to get home. I took a cab over here so I can ride home with you. I'll pick my car up in the morning, or have someone go and get it. I'm in no shape to drive."

That worried her more than anything. Cain loved to drive and he loved the little sports car she'd bought him as a wedding present. She was nearly bursting with the need to know when they slipped into the car and he closed the connection between them and the driver. The limo slid into traffic just as he started to talk.

"Remember me telling you about that young boy, Todd Whip? He came to see me today. I don't..." Cain leaned back on the seat as he continued. "He got his girlfriend pregnant and he wanted to know if I'd perform an abortion for her. She's going to a hack later in the week and he's worried for her safety."

Alyssa looked up at Cain. Her heart started pounding in her chest at the thought of what he might be thinking. She knew that she and Cain were trying to have a baby, but didn't know what his stand was on abortion. Before she could ask, he continued.

"She's twenty-five and should fucking know better." His voice was bitter and hard. "Todd is just a kid, nearly eight years her junior. What the hell was she thinking?

Todd said he thought he loved her, but now he's thinking she was using him. Alyssa, she wants him to kill her husband."

That startled her. Todd was only a kid, damn it. Then something occurred to her. Why did she want an abortion if she wanted Todd to kill her husband?

"That's his punishment because he refused to do what she wanted him to do." Cain growled as he went on. "She told him that if he couldn't help set her free, then he didn't deserve to know his kid. Stupid bitch. To do that to some...some kid is beyond cruel."

Alyssa agreed. "Do you think she's really pregnant, Cain? I mean, if she wants Todd to kill her husband, then she would be the type of person to lie about a baby too."

"Yeah, I thought about that too. Apparently, so did Todd. He's a smart kid, a lot smarter than I gave him credit for. He wants me to do the abortion so I can see if she really is. Then he asked about the police." He looked at her as he took her hand. "I want us to help him."

"Of course we will. What can we do besides calling Cait Grant?" Alyssa pulled out a pad of paper from her purse. "He'll need to be somewhere safe until this thing is over. And then we'll need to make sure... What are you doing? Don't just sit there like a bump on the log, call Cait Grant."

Cait was the Chief of Police. She was also a good friend of the family, and married to Spencer Grant. Spencer was a professor at the university and an all around good guy. Alyssa knew that if anyone could help, it would be Cait.

"I've already called her and Spence. We're having dinner with them tomorrow night at our house. Todd is coming by to look at my old car. I'm going to sell it to him cheap."

Alyssa grinned. Smart husband this man of hers. "And what am I going to do? I hope you know I'm not going to sit idly by and watch you have all the fun. If he's as good a kid as he seems, I want to help him too."

Cain's grin had her shudder. It was both sexy and hungry at the same time. She suddenly knew that he was no longer thinking about the young Todd and instead was thinking about her. She felt her body respond to him.

"I want you, Alyssa. I want you right now. Lean back on the seat and I'll show you just how much."

She felt her panties soak and her nipples harden. Damn, this man could make her go from normal to hot in a matter of nanoseconds. But she wanted to touch him first. Shaking her head at him, she reached for his cock, which was hard and thick.

"My turn. Lean back against the seat, big boy. I'm going to take your cock into my mouth first. Then if you can hold off until we get home, I'll ride you like you've never been ridden before."

His hiss of approval made her pussy gush again. Sliding down on the seat and then to the floor between his legs, Alyssa looked up at him. She unbuckled his belt as he pulled his shirt up. Easing the zipper down, she kissed the area as she exposed his skin.

"I've thought about this all day, taking you into my mouth, tasting you." Alyssa pulled his cock free of his pants and licked up the length of him. "Thinking about making you suffer like you did me last night. Making you ache like you made me ache and need."

"You loved it and you know it." His voice was rough and low. Glancing at her watch, she grinned at him. She had forty minutes and she was going to enjoy this.

~~~

Taking Sin to the airport the next afternoon had Cain thinking about how much he wished they all lived here again. He missed his sisters and now with Alyssa, he found he wanted to spend even more time with them. He said as much to Sin when he was alone with her.

"I'm making a career out of this, big brother, and as much as I love you, the thought of spending much time with you and Alyssa…well, let's just say that it's a little too much for one person to handle."

He flushed. "We're newlyweds. Of course we like to spend time with each other. Someday it will happen to you and I plan to tease you about it as well."

She laughed, that full, throaty one that made men turn and stare, and women as well. Sin was the epitome of her name.

"First of all, never going to happen. I don't care for men all that much that I'd want to spend more than an hour or two with them if I'm not scratching some itch. Secondly, and more importantly, you two will be doing this for the rest of your lives. Enjoy her and yourself. Leave me be, all right?" She kissed his cheeks and it took some of the bite out of her statement. "I love you, Cain."

He nodded and told her he loved her too. But he wasn't sure which bothered him more, the comment about not happening to her or the itch part. He decided not to touch either one. When her plane took off, he and Alyssa stood and watched the dot become smaller and smaller until it was nothing in the sky.

"I like her. She's a lot like you and Quinn, but more so. Did she tell you that she doesn't plan on ever marrying?" Alyssa asked as they left the airport.

Cain looked down at his wife. He wasn't sure why it surprised him that she knew. Alyssa and Sin had spent a great deal of time together last night and this morning just talking. He was glad that Alyssa loved his sisters because they loved her as well.

"I have an appointment with Drew in an hour," Alyssa said as they got into his car. "We're going to go over the Peabody account and then I have a meeting with the new employees at the store. What do you have planned for the day?"

"My mother. She wants to talk to me about the money situation that my father left her in. Then I have a late day at the clinic. Are you coming over later?"

Alyssa crinkled her nose. She and Guinevere Waite didn't get along. Cain supposed that was an understatement. His mother still blamed Alyssa for the death of Cain's father, Roscoe.

Roscoe had kidnapped and threatened to kill Quinn if Alyssa didn't give him two million dollars. When he'd tried to kill Cait Grant, she'd opened fire on him and killed him and his partner. It wasn't Alyssa's fault, of course, but his mother didn't care. She seemed to think that it was, including the kidnapping, because she hadn't given him the money in the first place. Money that he would have squandered before demanding more.

"Okay, then I'll meet you at home. I love you." And she slipped out of the car in front of the Howard building.

Cain drove to the hotel where his mother was staying. He didn't invite her to their home, but he did pay for her stay. He shuddered to think what would happen if they were all under the same roof. Besides, he loved having their home all to themselves.

The Howard estate was huge, as was the house. Just after Cain and Alyssa returned from their honeymoon several months ago, they'd moved in. Her mother had been staying there prior and it needed a major overhaul. Mother and daughter didn't have anywhere near the same tastes in anything. Then there were the changes that had been made. Locks, security, and the staffing as well, as they had put in a solarium off the third story master bedroom.

The house was massive at over fourteen thousand square feet of home. Upon entering the stunning two-story grand foyer, there was the spiral staircase that went up two more levels to the bedrooms and master suite on the uppermost floor. The master suite had its own safe room now, an exercise room, private patio, and sitting area. Huge walk-in cedar closets were bigger than his first apartment—hell, as big as the whole apartment building, he thought with a grin. The family area and the kitchen with a patio were their favorite places to start their day together with its views of the gardens out back. Alyssa said her father loved this area more than any other in the whole house. The family room with its three-story vaulted ceiling and access to the veranda looked down over the fireplace that was big enough to roast a hog or two in. The media room with another fireplace led the way to a cozy area for family and guests if they ever wanted to entertain.

The work shop and utility room off the first floor was his domain and he loved going in there and working on the old cars that Nathan, Alyssa's father, had never gotten around to finishing. The man had loved to tinker so it seemed, and had every tool imaginable to do it with. Cain loved this part of the house as well. There were spiral stairs in the veranda and stairs in the grand foyer to go up to the second floor. There were five bedrooms with private baths upstairs, as well as a large private retreat. Then there were the gardens.

The house was surrounded by over two hundred acres, mostly wooded areas, and a security fence went around the ten acres closest to the house. Their drive was private and a security team was out front twenty-four-seven. No one got in without permission, and that was seldom given unless he or Alyssa allowed it. His sisters, Drew, and his grandda Thomas, were the only ones who could come and go as they needed.

Pulling up in front of the hotel, Cain's phone rang. Smiling, he answered.

"Hello, Damon. How's retirement treating you? Is Charlotte driving you nuts yet?"

Last month, Damon Grant had retired. He'd been threatening it for some weeks now and Cain was surprised when the man, a dedicated doctor himself and Cain's mentor, actually did it.

"We're having a blast, my boy. Thanks for the cruise. Tell Alyssa that we love it. I need to ask a favor. Not a biggy, just something that I've just thought of."

He'd been just thinking of things nearly every day since he left, but Cain smiled. The man had given him this practice and had also been very helpful in his career as a doctor.

"Of course. You know I'd do anything for you and Charlotte. Name it." And he knew that he would too. The man was everything to him.

"I need you to arrange something for me. Charlotte and I will be back on the seventh and I want to make sure that the house is ready for us. Do you think you could please do that for us? Don't have a clue what that might involve, never had much say in the house anyway once I married, but there you have it. Not that I'm a chauvinist, but you might want to see what your lovely wife has to say on the matter. She had to do her own home and she probably has a hint or two to lend you."

Cain laughed. Alyssa was the least domestic person he knew and Damon knew it. If Cain wanted a hot meal and she was in the kitchen, she'd more likely than not tell him to microwave his cornflakes. He was very happy for the cooks they had on staff.

"I'll do that. I'll have someone pick you both up as well if you let me know when your plane lands. Then when you settle, we'll get together for dinner. You can show us your pictures."

After getting that settled Cain made a note on his phone and he got out of the car. His mother was waiting in the lobby, and she didn't look any happier to see him than he did her.

"Mother. We were going to meet in your room. What's going on?" He kissed her cheek and then helped her pull her jacket on.

"That room is a pigsty. I swear there are bugs as big as a cat in there. You'll have to put me up somewhere else or at that house of yours. I'm sure that the girls wouldn't mind moving out so that I can have some privacy. It's too nice of a house for them anyway. Besides, I'm thinking of moving back here permanently and I could make that my home as easily as any other, I suppose." She made it sound as if the house wasn't up to her standards.

"No. You can move back to Ohio if you want, but you do so on your own. The house belongs to me and I will not ask my sisters to move. As for this hotel, I own it as well with Alyssa and it's one of the nicest ones in the state. If it's not to your standard, then find other accommodations on your own or go back to California. It's entirely up to you."

He let her glare as he led her out to the car. He would take her to dinner, hear what she had to say, and send her on her way. If only it were that easy.

"I've been evicted from my house. I've nowhere to go. I have to come here or I live in a box."

So not what he wanted to hear.

CHAPTER 5

Drew sat in his office staring at the wall. He hadn't started out doing that, it was just what he kept finding himself doing. He picked up the stress ball off his desk and began tossing it into the air and catching it.

Quinn had kissed him. Not just kissed him, but really, really kissed him. He moaned again. With a quick swipe of his tongue he imagined that he could still taste her. He couldn't, he knew. They'd kissed…she'd kissed him yesterday. He frowned at that thought again.

He'd kissed her as well, though he wasn't about to admit how much he'd enjoyed it, and her. The way her body felt pressed against his, her breast, heavy and full, filling his hand. Drew threw the ball across the room and it hit the wall with a resounding crash. When it came back at him with a velocity that startled him he had to duck or be hit with it. Picking up the ball, he dropped it in his desk drawer. The knock at the door had him grimace. His secretary had heard it, he just knew. When Alyssa walked in he wasn't sure if he was annoyed or happy to see her.

"Dickhead Peabody is going to drive me nuts before this merger is over. He has more demands. Can't he just graciously leave me alone and let me purchase that heap of brick and be done with it?"

Drew grinned. "I hope you didn't call him dickhead when you asked. What does he want now, more time or more money?"

Arnold Peabody owned seven buildings in the downtown area. Four of which needed to be torn down before they fell on someone, one that had a nice location but needed extensive work, and the last two were what they really wanted.

They were old warehouses that sat on the same street across from each other. The Peabody Building, aptly named for the company that had started there making pottery of all things. It was three floors of hard maple and birch. The windows, long since broken out, were huge and would require a great deal of money to replace, but once finished, the rooms would shine with light. Alyssa was going to turn it into luxury studio apartments on the top two floors and shops and restaurants on the lower levels.

The March Building, a huge, sprawling building that covered an entire three square city blocks was just as beautiful and needed minimal work done to get it moving in the direction Alyssa had planned for it. The six-story building was going to be another office location for Howard Enterprises. Workers were going to convert the top level into Alyssa's office suite. She had already picked out the architect to do the work.

The lower level was going to be off street parking. Drew liked this idea in that it was difficult to find parking downtown where he lived on the best of days. Alyssa had already told him that he could use the garage if he needed to. He needed to.

The second and third floors were slated to become the law and accounting offices. With all the extra projects that the Howard Company was involved in it made sense to have departments dedicated to each area of expertise. Drew would be the head of this department.

The fifth floor was going to house the Howard Foundation. It had become too much for one person to manage and Alyssa had agreed with him in expanding it along with the area they needed to work in. At last count there were over three hundred people working in that department alone.

"He wants a piece of the pie, he said. What pie? It's going to cost millions to get the buildings up to code and then there are the ones that will have to be torn down. I wonder if he has any idea how much that's going to cost. Doubtful." She flopped down in the chair across from his desk.

She was barefooted again, he noticed. Usually, she would have a pair of shoes in his office in the event that someone needed her and she was unshod again. He grinned when he thought about the cost she must be saving on shoes.

"I'll give him a call." He glanced at the list he'd made before he'd gotten side tracked thinking about the kiss. "It's on my list of things to do anyway. Any word from that idiot in North Dakota yet?"

"No, and it's South, not North. He is supposed to be here next month. And he's not an idiot. He happens to be the world's best…" Stopping, she looked at him sharply. "What is the matter with you? You look…I don't know, like maybe you've been kicked in the balls."

Leave it to Alyssa to say what she thought. "I do not, I'm pensive. Big difference. And it's personal. I know you find it hard to believe that I have anything remotely resembling a personal life what with the hours you make me put in, but I do."

Her snort made him smile. There was something about working for the richest woman, no, the richest person in the world and knowing that she snorted that made a man's day. He vowed to make her do it more often.

"What is it this time? Is it the City Council, or is it the Mayor's office? I know, it's Quinn again."

He looked up at her and as soon as he did, he knew that he'd given himself away. Her eyes narrowed at him before she spoke.

"What is it about you two that makes you go at each other like cats and dogs? Maybe you should just get l—"

"Don't go there." He knew there was a bite to his words, but he couldn't stop it. "Let it go, Alyssa. It's just something she and I have to work out."

Alyssa was quiet for a few minutes and in that time, Drew shifted in his seat twice. She got up, walked to his fridge, and knelt down to it. He was more nervous now than if he was facing a room full of angry citizens like he had last week over the proposed closing of the Book Nook.

"Alyssa, say something." He wasn't sure what he wanted her to say, but knew that if she didn't, he'd never be able to think straight.

"She's had a hard life. Not just with her father, though that man was a peach. No, she was married once, and he was…he hit her."

"I would never hit her, you have to know that." Drew was hurt and insulted that she would even say that.

"I know that, dumbass. I'm telling you why she might be putting you off if you have feelings for her. His name was Wicket, Carl Wicket. I don't know that much about him, only what she and the others have said, but he wasn't a man. No man would do that to a woman and be expected to be one."

"She isn't the problem. She…aw fuck, Alyssa, she kissed me." He got up and started pacing behind her. "And not anything brotherly either. I don't know what to do about it, or her. She threw me out of her office right after. I might have…I did piss her off."

He'd already told Cain and figured the man would tell his wife. He had told him not to and was surprised that he hadn't. His respect for the man just raised a few more notches.

"We were fighting. Again. And she just reached out and pulled me to her. I was as surprised as you look right now. But then it changed. The kiss, I mean. And I got greedy. I didn't mean to, but…then I realized who she was and what she was to me." Alyssa didn't say anything for a while and he looked over to her. She was laughing. Not just laughing, but tears streaming down her face laughing. Drew failed to see the humor in his situation. "What the fuck, Alyssa? I'm pouring out my misery to you and you're hysterical. Thanks a whole fucking lot."

It took her several more minutes to stop long enough to talk to him and in that time, Drew felt angrier. He was about to leave her to her fun when she finally regained control.

"You're not related to her, are you?" Drew shook his head. "Then what's the problem? Go for it. She's beautiful, single, and obviously likes you. Unless of course you're gay. Not that it matters, I suppose, but you know—"

"No, I'm not gay. Damn it, you're supposed to be pissed because I'm dating the family. Not tell me to 'go for it.' This isn't a pair of shoes, this is…this is…I don't know what the fuck it is, but it is." He glared at her again. "Damn it, stop laughing."

That stopped her. She stood up and walked to him. He was sure she was going to slug him. She'd hit a man before in a board meeting a few weeks ago. Drew felt he deserved it more than the moron who had tried to grope her under the table. She put her hands on his shoulders and smiled. He was in deeper than he thought.

"You are just as much family to us as Quinn. And I'm sort of insulted that you would think I'd give two shits about you dating one of the 'family.' Your grandda is like a father to me…well, a grandfather, and you mean a great deal to me as well. Date her, marry her, I don't care, but stop making yourself miserable over something that means nothing to anyone but you."

Without thought, he kissed her. He might have gotten away with it except Quinn chose that moment to walk in on them. No one moved for several seconds. Then Quinn backed out without a word and closed the door behind her.

Alyssa looked up at him. "Well, go after her, you big idiot." And he did.

~~~

Quinn heard him say her name, but she ignored it. As well as she could with him nearly at her heels. She tried to speed up, but her shoes were slowing her down. Kicking them off, she took off at a run and was feeling like she'd make it when he closed his hand over her elbow and followed her into her office.

"Get out, I don't think I want to—"

"No," he said as he shut the door behind them. "It's not what you think. Actually, I don't know what you're thinking, but it's not as nefarious as you seem to think it is. I was just kissing her."

"I'm well aware of what you were doing. You were kissing my brother's wife. How could you? You work for…you'll kiss Alyssa and not—"

Whatever else she might have been going to say was cut off by his mouth. The bite of it, the hard pressure made her groan. At least that's what she tried to tell herself. But he felt so good, so right. When he changed the angle of his head and wrapped his arm around her to pull her closer, Quinn couldn't think at all.

His body was hard against hers. His muscles bunched and moved under her fingers when she moved them up and over his shoulders. When Drew nipped at her lower lip, seemingly asking for permission to enter her mouth, she let him. The taste of him exploded in her mouth and her senses.

She wanted to touch him, to feel if his skin felt anywhere near what she thought it should. Moving her fingers to the buttons down the front of his shirt, she was nearly ready to rip it from him when he pulled back. She whimpered slightly before she could stop it.

"I'm not going anywhere. I want you to unbutton my shirt, Quinn. Please, baby, undress me."

His voice was husky and low. It sent shivers down her body and into her core. She was suddenly glad she'd kicked off her shoes because she was positive that she wouldn't be able to stand up on them.

When his first button was undone, she leaned in and kissed the exposed area. He tasted hot and spicy, his skin warm and firm. When he leaned back more and braced his hands on either side of her, she unbuttoned two more and licked him. His moan made her look up at his face.

"Don't stop, Christ, don't stop now. You're making me crazy with need, but I don't want you to stop." He leaned in and took her mouth in a hungry kiss. "Finish me."

Moving the next button from its tiny hole, she moved his shirt over enough to find his nipple. It was as hard as hers felt and she couldn't resist taking the small brown disk into her mouth and nipping him. His fingers threading into her hair had her held in place. Not that she wanted to move. When his groin moved against her, a hard thrust over and over into her hips, she gripped his waist and threw back her head.

"Please, Drew, I need you to…please?" She didn't know what she wanted him to do most, touch her, kiss her, or simply take her to the floor and take her. When his hand slid up her thigh and under her skirt, she shifted her legs apart, wanting him to touch her heat. She was very glad she'd opted to not wear hose today and may not ever again.

His fingers moved along the seam of her ass and then further down. When he was at her entrance, she moaned again. Then he entered her, his finger moving inside. He buried his face in her neck and nipped.

"I want you, Quinn, right now. But we can't. I don't have any protection. Baby, please, I'm sorry." His thigh slipped between her legs and he lifted her against him. "Come for me, Quinn. Come please."

She couldn't have stopped if her life depended on it. Her body didn't just respond to his command, but detonated. His mouth covered hers and muffled her screams. Over and over her body peaked; wave after wave washed over her until she was sure she would die from it. When he commanded her to come again, she did, riding his fingers and his thigh hard until she was spent.

Neither of them moved. Quinn could feel his cock and wanted more than anything to give him the same pleasure he'd given her. Moving her hand down his front to his zipper, he stopped her with his hand covering hers.

"If you do that, I'll come. And for as much as I'd like to right now, I have nothing to wear for the rest of the day." She wanted to laugh, but all she could think of was his cock coming all over her.

He didn't move his head, which was still lying heavily against her neck, and he bit her gently. She giggled. Instead of lifting his head, he turned to look at her.

"I don't find this all that funny, love. I've got the worst case of blue balls known to man. Giggling at a man in this much pain is just cruel."

Before she could answer, which she was sure would make him be in more pain, someone knocked on her door.

"Quinn, it's Alyssa. Have you seen Drew?" Both Quinn and Drew burst out laughing.

CHAPTER 6

Shannon Howard sat in the diner and looked at the man across from her. Samuel Howard, her brother-in-law and sometime lover, was not in the best of humor. When Guinevere Waite had asked them to meet her here she said she had something to talk about. Nothing she could say could be worth sitting one more second in this hovel. Shannon was ready to leave.

"She's not even technically late yet. It's only fifteen after. You show up at least an hour late for things and expect people to wait for you." Samuel leaned back in the booth.

"I am not late, I'm fashionably on time. There's a difference when you have money." Well, used to have money. "She is doing this just to piss me off and we both know it. What could that person possibly say to me that she couldn't say over the phone?"

Samuel didn't say anything, but his look, that look of incredulity, said it all. Shannon wasn't going to dignify it with any answer. She had been avoiding the incessant phone calls and the annoying little notes for weeks now. The woman's husband tried to kill his own child, what could she possibly think they could have in common?

"She has five more minutes then I'm leaving. I have a hair appointment at eleven that I can't possibly be late for. And I have that meeting with my daughter."

"You have a meeting with Alyssa? Since when?" Samuel looked shocked and that made Shannon angrier.

"I told you that I was seeing her today. I've told you twice already. She needs to loosen the purse strings more. I can't possibly live on that little income and do the things I need to do. Why, she embarrassed me to death last week when I went to the Country Club and they told me that my membership hadn't been paid." Shannon shifted on the vinyl and wondered again why they didn't have special seats made of real leather for when people of money came in.

"And that...that house," Shannon shuddered. "I've seen better accommodations in those pet hotels. I plan to tell her that I've had enough of her treating her mother this way."

Samuel snorted. "She'll just tell you to get a job again. Just like she has the last six times you've gone there to see her. And if you think that guy in the lobby is going to let you in then you're crazier than that son of yours."

Shannon started to tell him that Nathan wasn't crazy but depressed. And he wasn't just her son, but Samuel's as well. The poor boy had been through so much. But he'd been absolutely no help when she'd asked him to be. Imagine a drug addict not knowing what to use to knock someone… She wasn't going to think about that disaster right now.

Shannon was still surprised that her late husband and Alyssa's father had figured out that the boys weren't his. She'd been surprised to find that Robert wasn't, but Nathan? She'd known right from the beginning that he hadn't been her husband's. And the nerve of him blaming her for her having those affairs. If he'd spent more time at home instead of with his fucking daughter then she wouldn't have had to seek her sex from others. He had dropped that bombshell on her at the reading of the will.

The door to the diner opened and in walked Guinevere. Shannon tried not to gawk, but the woman had no fashion sense at all. And her hair…Shannon wondered if the woman cut it herself and then thought that it went well with her choice of clothing.

It wasn't as if she was dressed in a jogging suit, it's just that Shannon thought she should at least dress for the people she was associating with. Her hair was the least of her complaints. There was the fact that her makeup was cheap. No one should buy their cosmetics at a drug store. There, she'd said it. Guinevere must have purchased her cosmetics there along with her attire.

Then her clothes, she was wearing the wrong season for her skin tone and she was wearing no lipstick. How a woman could even think of leaving the house without a bit of lipstick was beyond her. Shannon actually reached for her bag to give her a tube of hers when she remembered that she had to get more money before she started giving poor women her eighty-five-dollar a tube colorant.

"I'm sorry I'm late, but I had a horrible morning. Just horrible. I had to go and see my son and he was no help. Not that he ever has been. You'd think bringing a person into this world would make them have some respect for their parents, wouldn't you? Then my daughters…well, I don't need to tell you how ungrateful daughters can be." She flopped down in the plastic chair and picked up her menu. "Have you ordered yet? I just love the food here."

"Ummm, no. We were…I'm not hungry." Shannon stole a glance at Samuel and nearly burst out laughing at the look on his face. "You go ahead. Don't let us stop you."

"Oh, that's too bad. Oh well, I'll just have something light." Guinevere opened her menu and when the waitress came back with a water and coffee, Guinevere ordered what amounted to half of one side of the page.

When she had her juice and her first course she took out a notebook and pen and opened it to the first page. "I want you to help me get back at our children. They need to be taught a lesson. There is no reason for them to treat us as if we didn't bring them into this world."

~~~

Quinn and Drew moved along the hallway toward the conference room without looking at each other. Quinn wanted to see his face; actually, she wanted to see all of him, but was terrified to admit it. She still couldn't believe what they had done, what she had done in her office. Heat infused her face again.

Alyssa's timing was perfect, or not. Depending on which minute she was asked, Quinn might give a different answer every time. She wanted her to have not come to the door and she wished that she'd been a few minutes earlier. Quinn wished that she had let Drew take her to the floor and she wished that she had been sterner about him leaving her office. Her head was beginning to hurt. Taking a quick glance over at Drew Quinn thought he didn't look any happier.

What had she been thinking? Sex with her sister-in-law's lawyer? In her office? Against the door? Christ, she was never going to live this down if it ever got out. She had to make sure that no one found out, anyone. Especially not Alyssa. Or her brother. Holy shit, Cain would kill her. And then Drew. She was so deep in thought that Quinn nearly walked by the door that Alyssa and Drew had gone into.

"I need to get this done," Alyssa said as soon as the door closed behind them. "I've put it off for weeks now and I can't any longer. I need to get someone in my outer office that is permanent. I know that the people working there have been…what's wrong?"

Quinn looked over at Drew who was looking at Alyssa. *She knew* was the first thing that popped into her head. The gossip had already found out and it was all over the company now. Quinn started to stand up to tell Alyssa what had happened, but Drew stopped her with a hand to her arm.

"What do you mean? Nothing's wrong," he stated as he continued to look at Alyssa. "I think this is a great idea. You can't keep retraining another new secretary every week. It's good practice for the employees, but you need someone who can give you a daily counting of your appointments, not take your time up while you train them on your calendar."

"I know that, but I like helping them. It's very rewarding. But you're also right about it taking up a lot of my time. And I need to devote more time at home too." Alyssa looked at them both. "Any suggestions?"

Quinn was nodding, though her heart was tight. All she could think about was Drew and what they had done. What he thought they were going to do.

She looked over at him and nearly groaned out loud. His buttons were all wrong. Not only that, but she was sure Alyssa knew it. It was the small little hesitation in her speech then laughter burbled out. Laying her head on the table, Quinn suddenly wanted them all to go away. When she felt someone run their fingers through her hair, she was disappointed when she lifted her head and found Alyssa there.

"He went to get me a list of qualified applicants. I told him to take his time." Quinn sat up and stared at Alyssa. "You want to talk about it?"

Did she? No. Yes. Hell, she didn't know. Quinn got up to pace.

"He kissed me," Quinn blurted out, then couldn't seem to shut up. "Well, I kissed him first then he...I didn't think he wanted me. Then he did. Then I don't. Now...we didn't have any protection and you knocked on the door."

"I see. Well, not really. Did you want him to have protection?" Leave it to Alyssa. "I mean, is that why you're upset with him?"

"No. I didn't want him to have pro...I didn't want him to have a reason to...damn it, I don't know what I want."

She started to cry and felt stupid. "He's so beautiful, isn't he? And smart too. Why would he want—"

"Don't you dare finish that sentence," Alyssa snapped before Quinn could finish. "Why would he want you? Well, let's see, you're beautiful, both inside and out. You're reasonably smart. I thought you were smarter until you started saying crap like you just were. Then you're sexy." Quinn snorted at her. "And you have the manners of a trucker. Will you look at yourself? You're probably too good for him."

Quinn giggled, which is what she was sure Alyssa meant for her to do. "I hate him most of the time."

"And the rest of the time," Alyssa asked with a laugh. "Don't answer that. Quinn, you're an adult he's an adult. If either of you or both of you want to have monkey sex on your desk, I say go for it. Cain and I certainly do it often enough."

Quinn looked at her. "So did not want to hear that. The thought of my brother…well, let's just say that I can think of millions upon millions of things I'd like better than to think of sex and Cain."

A knock at the door had them both turn to it. Drew walked in and looked at her. Quinn blushed at the way he just stared at her and all she could think about was sex on her desk. Lots of sex on her desk with him. She blushed again. Damn, she wanted to kill Alyssa for putting that thought in her head.

Quinn's phone twittered, signaling she had a text. Excusing herself, she went to see what her department wanted now. She probably could have taken it there, but needed to get out for a few minutes.

CHAPTER 7

Shannon sat in the lobby, looked around, and didn't see a clock. She glanced at her watch again and decided that her daughter was the rudest woman she'd ever known. She had to know that her mother was down here waiting and was being facetious about it.

So what if she didn't have an appointment? Not that anyone would let her make one anyway. This was as far as she ever got when she came to this building to see her—the lobby. Trying to look as bored as possible when she wanted to stand and scream, Shannon thought about what Guinevere suggested at the restaurant this morning.

She didn't agree with the woman. Only an insane person would believe that kidnapping their children and demanding ransom was going to work. But some of what she'd said of the other plan had made sense.

Suing her, demanding that Alyssa pay her for pain and suffering had its merits. And Shannon had suffered, she thought. She had gone from an endless supply of money to being reduced to begging for table scraps to get by. She didn't have her driver and her car, there were no more trips to the spa when she needed them, and forget the luncheons she would host for all her friends. All that was a thing of the past, but not anymore.

And then there were no credit cards, no cash in her pocketbook. Not that she ever used cash, but knowing it was there was the point. Her hair wasn't done by a stylist anymore that came to her house, but one that she had to go to. And she was still wearing last year's castoffs, or they would be as soon as she could buy this year's style.

Shannon looked at her watch again. She'd been here for three hours now and she would wait her out if it killed her. She wanted to stick her tongue out at the people at the security desk, but she didn't dare. She was afraid they'd toss her out again like they had every other time she'd come here.

She thought about her son Nathan. He was adjusting to this forced life style, she supposed. He was in a rehab center that specialized in his type of sickness. Shannon refused to think of it as an addiction. He was just going through some issues and would soon be up on his feet. That was another thing that Alyssa had taken from her. Nathan wasn't in the posh place he'd been before, but one that actually followed the rules. She hadn't seen her son in over three months. And when she'd gone there demanding to see her baby, they'd called the police. She wasn't even sure when he was going to be released.

And if she thought Nathan was living with her and Samuel then she had another thought coming. Their house wasn't large enough for him as well as his friends. She loved her son, but she had to draw the line sometime.

Having Robert there was bad enough with his temper, but the two of them…no, she wouldn't have that.

That would have to change too. The living arrangements were just too cramped and too beneath them all. Shannon pulled out her little notebook and noted that in it. Shannon gave an indelicate snort. House indeed. It was barely more than a hovel with its five bedrooms and three-car detached garage. The dining room was hardly big enough for twenty guests when she entertained—which hadn't been much. Her friends were just too busy this time of year and frankly, she was ashamed to bring anyone there.

Then was no pool either. When she'd pointed that out to her ungrateful daughter, Alyssa claimed that Shannon didn't swim so it would be a waste of money. Everyone who was anyone had a pool, but Alyssa wouldn't budge. She told her if she wanted one, then to pay for it herself. Of course she would…and pigs would fly. But Robert was not happy and when he wasn't happy then he was—

"Mrs. Howard? Mrs. Waite said to tell you she isn't going to see you today."

Shannon startled when the man touched her arm to get her attention.

"She suggested that you make an appointment like everyone else."

"But I've been here for three hours. I need to see her. Tell her that as her mother, I demand that she come down here this instant. I've been put off—" Four men in security uniforms and guns stepped up behind the man speaking.

"As I was saying," the man said with a smirk, "you need to make an appointment. These gentlemen will see you out." The man walked away, leaving the others standing there.

Shannon didn't say anything. She'd been literally tossed out on her ass before by these "gentlemen" and she wasn't going through that again. She tried to hold onto her anger as well as she could and not give these men any reason to grab her, but it was difficult. By the time she had been escorted to her car and she got buckled in her head was pounding. She'd had enough.

~~~

Alyssa stood at the window and watched her mother be escorted out. It hurt her to see this, but she'd had no choice. When a woman tried to drug her own daughter to make her have sex with her uncle, things were a lot harder to forgive and forget. Her mother made her own bed and now she had to lie in it. Turning away from the window, she sat back at her desk.

Her mother and uncle had drugged her when she'd been seventeen. Her father had only been gone a few short weeks, having died of a heart attack, and they had just read the will. Alyssa had inherited everything. All the money—billions of it—the houses, over a dozen of them all over the world, and her family, but all she wanted was her daddy back.

Shannon was mad because Alyssa's dad had known about the affairs and that neither Nathan the fourth nor her other brother Robert were her full brothers. She was his only child and the only one to inherit. Alyssa was also responsible for her mother and brothers' wellbeing. She was to provide them with so much money a year for twenty years; a crock of shit, Drew had called it. But that hadn't worked the way her daddy wanted.

She had met them at the restaurant when her mother asked and had been drugged. Their plan had been to have her uncle Samuel get her pregnant and she would have no choice but to let them continue on the way they had been. But Alyssa had run away from the restaurant to be hidden away for nearly ten years.

If it hadn't been for Cain and his sisters Alyssa wasn't sure how much longer she would have stayed away. Alyssa reached for the bottled water and went through the ritual of checking it.

The drugs had been in her tea glass. And to this day, she could only drink bottled water after she checked for pin holes and broken seals. It's not that she didn't trust anyone, but old habits die hard. She smiled when she thought of her husband and his inventive ways of trying to get her to drink out of a glass again. He was a wonderful, sexy man. Alyssa's phone ringing had her reaching for it before she remembered her secretary.

"Howard Corporation, how can I help you?" She winced when she saw Quinn come in the door with her hand on her hip. With a whispered "Sorry," she listened to the voice at the other end.

"Who is this?" the caller demanded. "I'm looking for Alyssa, that rich woman. Can you tell me how to contact her?"

Alyssa put the phone on speaker and waved Quinn over.

"I've been trying for a damned month. I got an appointment with her and I've not been able to speak to her about it."

Quinn shook her head and pulled out her cell while Alyssa talked. "I'm sorry, sir, did you say you had an appointment? If you would just tell me your name then I could see where to direct your call. I know for a fact that appointments are—"

"What you should do, girly, is put the president on the line. I've got an appointment with her and she won't be none too pleased to know that I've been put off." He huffed at her. "As I've said, she's expecting me to call her."

Drew came in the door and he was on his phone as well. He was talking in hushed tones and handed Alyssa a note as he continued. "Keep him talking," was all it said. She raised a brow at him. Seriously, this was his advice? She rolled her eyes and spoke to the caller.

"Okay, tell me your name so that I can put the call through. Alyssa doesn't just let me put calls through to her unless I give her a name." Drew gave her a thumbs up. She was going to break it off when she got off this call, she decided. "And if you can give me a little information about what you had the appointment for, maybe that'll narrow it down for me."

The man on the phone huffed again. "I ain't doing your work for you. You just put me through the line and I'll try to speak kindly about you when I speak to her. I doubt it'll do you much good, but I'll give it my best."

Alyssa just bet he would. She debated for all of a minute then leaned back in her chair. Anger made people stupid and she was betting this guy had it in spades. The stupid part, she thought.

"No." She waited a full ten seconds before she continued. "No, I'm not putting you through, you pompous windbag. Appointment? Really? That's the best you can come up with?"

"Now you see here, you're not talking to me that way, young lady. I'll have you know that she and I go way…" He took a deep breath before continuing. "I'll not explain myself to you. Put the damned bitch on the fucking phone," he yelled at her.

Alyssa grinned. "My, my. You sure have changed your tune, haven't you? Not only do you not have an appointment, you probably can't spell appointment. What is your name?" she demanded right back.

"Brian Sa—" The line went dead. Alyssa pressed the speaker button to disconnect the humming noise.

She looked up at the several people now crowding her office. "I guess I made him mad. Does someone want to tell me what the fuck is going on?"

Quinn sat in the chair across from her and then Drew. The other people, mostly security, just milled about the room. Alyssa could ignore them for now. She wanted answers.

"Somebody called my office earlier this week," Quinn started. "He said he had some money he wanted to donate."

"I don't take donations, not unless it's at a fundraiser for another foundation. This company funds its own charities. What did he say he wanted to do with the money?" Alyssa was sure she wasn't going to like her answer.

"He got mad at me because I wouldn't give him any information about you. He wanted to speak to you and then when I refused, he hung up."

Alyssa sat back and looked at her. Quinn was upset, but so was she. She should have been informed about this. Then she realized that if she was informed about every crackpot that called in the offices, she'd never get anything done.

"Does Cain know?" Alyssa asked the two of them. At the shake of her head, she knew he'd be pissed when he did. "One of you has to tell him and don't be surprised when he has a fit. He's overprotective of me, in case you hadn't noticed."

"We got a trace on the call. I'm not sure if it was long enough, but with your money and my knowledge," Drew started with a grin, "we can do anything."

His phone rang and he got up to answer it. Alyssa looked at Quinn. She looked sad, depressed even. Alyssa got up from her desk and sat next to Quinn in the chair on the opposite side.

"Quinn? Look at me, sweetie." It took Alyssa touching Quinn's arm before she turned. "This isn't your fault. I'm a very wealthy woman; people are going to threaten me all the time."

"I know, but...Alyssa, I couldn't stand it if anything happened to you. You're more than a person married to my brother, you're my best friend."

The two women hugged and were still hugging when Drew came back. He didn't look happy.

"The call came from a 'pay as you go phone' and is more difficult to trace. Not impossible, but harder. I'm sorry, ladies, we'll get him. Sooner or later, we'll get him."

Alyssa hoped so. She had enough on her plate right now. She didn't need some idiot threatening her.

CHAPTER 8

Cain was pissed. On top of everything else, his wife had a crackpot calling her office. He paced the bedroom again and looked up when Alyssa walked out of the bathroom. She'd been crying; he could see the tear stains on her cheeks and her red nose.

"Oh, baby. I'm sorry. Come here and let me hold you." He gathered her into his arms. "This thing will work out, you'll see. Some idiot with more time than sense is all it is."

"You don't believe that anymore than I do. But this isn't just about that guy. My mother came by again today." She sat in one of the chairs by the fireplace. "I had her escorted out again. When will she just give it up and move on with her life?"

Their families, especially the mothers, were a piece of work. And getting more and more difficult to deal with daily. Cain sat next to her in the other chair and wondered if Shannon Howard would give up either. She was a fool if she thought she could wear her daughter down. Alyssa was the most stubborn woman he knew.

"Yeah, mine came by too. She's been evicted from her home in California for nonpayment of rent. She wanted me to set up a house for her." Cain snorted. "Like I'll jump right on that one after what she did to you and Quinn."

Neither of them spoke for a while and Cain looked over and saw that Alyssa was asleep. He watched her for as long as he could then got up and answered the door when someone knocked.

"Your guests have arrived, sir. And there is also a young man in the kitchen who says you asked him to come by." Carol glanced at Alyssa who was in the chair behind him. "Shall I turn them away? The young miss hasn't been sleeping all that well. I'm sure they'd understand."

It was tempting, but he knew that Alyssa would be angry if he did that. "Tell them we'll be right down. Oh, and Carol? Please make sure that the young man, Todd Whip, is taken in to be with Doctor and Captain Grant. And he's probably starving. I remember being that young and hungry all the time once."

With a small curtsy, the woman left. Cain turned to wake Alyssa and noticed that she was awake and looking at him with a strange smile.

"Do you think the household knows I'm not sleeping well?" She stood up and stretched. "Or just her?"

Cain couldn't think past the need and love for this woman that settled over him. He wanted to drag her to the bed and make love to her and he wanted to hold her until all the badness around them disappeared. It took him a few seconds to realize she was speaking.

"…away for a few days. I was thinking Paris again. We had so much fun there on our honeymoon. I have some things there I need to look at and we could make a mini vacation out of it." She looked at him and smiled. "Is sex all you ever think about?"

"Yes," he answered without a bit of hesitation. "Especially since I married you. As soon as our guests leave, I'm going to bring you back up here and show you."

Her sultry laugh followed them down the stairs and into the living room. Cain wasn't sure, but he thought his wife had, by far, the sexist laugh he'd ever heard. And he hoped to hear a great deal more of it.

Todd was nervous. Anyone could see it. He fidgeted and paced and when he wasn't doing that, he was pacing and fidgeting. Every time he sat down he'd pop back up like a spring-loaded game.

Cain didn't comment, but simply watched. Alyssa finally got up and sat on the couch where Todd would sit for a few seconds then resume his march around the room. Cain wondered what she was up to and thought that she was going to make it worse. The kids didn't seem to like women much right now.

"Come over here and sit down Todd." She patted the seat next to her on the couch. "I want to ask you about a job I might have for you."

Todd looked panicky, but sat. He was perched on the edge and watched Alyssa like she was going to attack him. It was all Cain could do not to laugh at his expression.

"What do you know about football?" He glanced at Cain when Alyssa asked. "I know a little bit, but not much. How much do you know?"

"Football? Yeah, okay. I like it. I played in biddy league until my mom couldn't afford it anymore." Todd glanced at Cain again. "Why?"

The suspicion in his voice was evident. Spencer started to laugh, but a sharp look from his wife had him coughing. Neither man, it appeared, wanted to piss off their wives.

"Have you heard of the Rodney Kincaid Clinic?" Alyssa asked him. Todd nodded. "Good. Well, there are a bunch of children that come there weekly with injuries from various sports. I was—"

"I didn't do it." Todd jumped up again, anger in his voice. "I don't even know those kids."

"Well of course you didn't do it. What a silly notion. Sit down." Todd sat. "I was wondering if you'd want a job organizing them. I have professionals coming in to help out, but the kids are backward or shy and won't sign up. I thought you could help out by encouraging them to step forward and take part. I hoped you'd enjoy that."

Todd stared at her. Cain continued the conversation with Spencer on who was going to the state championship in basketball, but still keeping an ear on the conversation going on behind him. Suddenly, Cait, Spencer's wife, got up and went to the couch too.

"What a marvelous idea, Alyssa. Todd, do you know much about basketball?" Cait sat on the other side of him. "My boys played basketball in high school. So did Meggie all the way through college."

"Meggie Grant? Meggie Grant is your daughter?" The awe in Todd's voice was evident. "I saw her play once. Wow, she's all that. Pretty too."

"Meggie is, isn't she? She wants to help out Alyssa too. You think you'd be willing to help her out as well with that sport?"

And just like that, Todd sat back on the couch and relaxed. By the time they all went into dinner Todd had a job, an office at the newly built rec center, and a car to drive himself back and forth to work. Cain looked over at Spencer as they followed Todd and the two women into the dining room.

"They're good. Boy didn't stand a chance against them, did he?" Spencer laughed before he continued. "I certainly didn't against a pretty girl at that age."

Cain laughed. "I still don't."

~~~

Quinn was watching TV when someone knocked on her bedroom door. She turned the set off and went to the door. She hoped it was just the housekeeper leaving, but knew she couldn't be that lucky. It was her sister Jazzie.

"Hey. I was wondering if you know anyone who was hiring? I need a job in the security field," Jazzie said as the barged into the room and flopped down on the bed. "That job with the restaurant didn't pan out. He wanted me to use three-day-old meat to cook and I didn't think that would be safe."

Jazzie was flighty. She couldn't hold down a job if her life depended on it. And she seemed to have the attention span of a goldfish. But Quinn loved her.

"No, not off the top of my head. You could just take the job Alyssa offered you and be working for a great boss. It's still open." And would stay so until Jazzie took the thing, as far as Alyssa was concerned.

Alyssa had opened the cafeteria in the main building and there were plans for ones in the new buildings as well. Jazzie would be perfect for the job as head baker. It was a great opportunity in that she'd be the only cook and Alyssa and the rest of the family could keep an eye on her.

"Nah, I don't do charity. How about that place on Winder? They just opened up and will need someone to watch over the place, won't they?" Jazzie asked hopefully.

Quinn sat on the bed. "And it's already closed down. Health department. And I don't think the job from Alyssa is charity. She wants you to be her cook and she will pay you."

Jazzie shook her head. "Let's order pizza. That guy who delivered last time was cute. I'll even let you pick the toppings." Jazzie was already scrambling for the phone as she spoke. "Pop too. Coke this time. And you pay. I'm unemployed."

Again, Quinn thought about her sister's state of employment, but knew better than to say it.

Her cell phone rang just as Jazzie reached for it and made them both jump back. Jazzie picked it up and opened it. "Quinn's house of ill repute. Tell us your pleasures and we'll make them happen." Jazzie's smile faded as she listened. "Sure, she's right here."

Quinn took the phone and put it to her ear. Hopefully whoever was on the other end had a sense of humor. It was Drew and he most certainly did not.

"What if I'd been a client? You should teach your sister to have respect for other people's phone calls and—" Quinn closed the phone then opened it and turned off the power.

"Is he mad?" Quinn looked at her sister. "I was only kidding around. Maybe you should tell him to get the pike out of his ass and learn to loosen up."

Quinn agreed. "Let's order that pizza, only this time let's use the house phone. And don't worry about Drew. He's pissed at me most of the time anyway."

The wine was opened as Jazzie ordered their dinner. While she ordered and flirted, that was. Quinn had one glass and was pouring the second when Jazzie hung up. Quinn decided to drown her sorrows and if that wouldn't work, she was going to get drunk—shit faced, as she'd heard it called.

She was having a shitty week and she'd worked hard to avoid Drew all week too. She had succeeded for the most part too. That was until today. The meeting with the department heads, the phone calls, then her meeting with the accounting department had had him at each one of them. Avoiding him there had been impossible.

The accounting department wanted more centralized ways to keep track of the monies being spent. They said that Alyssa's money was going out too quickly to be safe. Safe? Quinn didn't understand and asked what he had meant.

"It's her money, right? And I'm pretty sure she can spend it anyway she wants. Not to mention, she has like billions of it."

The accountant, Brian Santos, looked at her and shook his head. "Miss Waite, you don't seem to understand. We need to curtail her spending before she takes the company down with her and that just won't do. No, you need to tell her to stop spending it and to save. We wouldn't want to have to be broke by the end of the year now, would we, girly?"

Quinn walked away. It was that or shoot the man. She also made a note to have someone else go over the books. They didn't need someone like that working for them.

By the time the pizza arrived Quinn was on her third glass of wine, and well into her fourth when the bell rang again, signaling another guest. She drained it on the way to the door. She was giggling when she opened it and nearly took a tumble into the man's arms there. Drew. And when she looked up into his eyes, they were furious.

"You hung up on me. Then I couldn't reach you again. I don't appreciate you hanging up on me then turning off your phone. It's childish." He pushed his way past her when she tried to close the door on him. "We have things to discuss and I'm not going to be put off again. You've been avoiding me."

Quinn was pretty sure she was drunk because there was no way her mind could go where it did while he was standing there yelling at her. Carnal thoughts of sweaty bodies and crumpled sheets, clothes strewn about the room, her room, kept looping in her mind. She simply leaned in and buried her nose into his neck.

"Yummy, you smell so good. I think I'd like a taste." Quinn felt his hands on her arms the second she ran her tongue along his throat. "Yep, you taste as good as you smell."

"Quinn," he whispered, his voice tight. "What are you doing to me? This isn't…Christ, yes."

Quinn didn't know herself, but she liked it. Walking him back, she pressed him against the wall and then herself into him. He felt so good, hard and warm, smooth and silky. Need rushed her body when she felt his cock hard and thick against her belly as she covered her mouth over his.

CHAPTER 9

Drew was dizzy with the sensations she was creating in his body. He needed to get control or he was going to embarrass them both and take her right there where they stood. Turning them both around, he had her lifted up and her legs wrapped around his hips. Her mouth and tongue didn't stop moving. He was quickly losing it and he wasn't ready for that.

"Bedroom?" he asked against her throat. Even as he asked he was hoping it was close. If it wasn't, then all bets were off and she was going to be under him soon.

"Stairs. Left. Hurry."

They stopped twice to taste, to touch, and to feel. Drew was on fire for her, his body needing hers like a drug. Once they were in the room he nearly dropped her to the floor and took her then. She'd freed his cock before they'd had the door open and was making him hurt with her hands wrapped around him. He was seconds from coming.

"Please, Drew. I need you." With her legs still wrapped around him, he lowered them to the bed. He tore open her blouse; buttons flew everywhere. Cupping her breast in his palm, Drew covered the silk-covered orb with his mouth, his teeth nipping hard at her nipple he could feel beneath. Her body arched up, her fingers curled in his hair.

There was no time for foreplay. Besides, as far as Drew was concerned, their whole relationship had been leading up to this. She was driving him to the edge quicker now. Running his hands up under her skirt, he felt silk and flesh, thigh-highs and a thong. Drew grabbed the fabric and tore it from her body as he freed her breast. Reason was gone, need pounded at him. His cock poised at her entrance, Drew lifted his head to ask her if it was safe when she lunged up and took him.

She was tight, wet, and hot. As soon as he rocked into her core she came screaming his name. Her sheathed tightening around him brought him with her. Throwing back his head, Drew roared out his release. He was both happy and disappointed that he'd not been able to see and taste more of her.

Drew couldn't move after he dropped onto her. He finally managed to roll them over, her body spread over his a few minutes later. But if he needed to do anything else, he was sunk.

Quinn Waite lay over him. Looking down at her sleeping face, he still couldn't believe it. Christ, she was passionate. And his body was already stirring for another taste of her, longer this time, he hoped.

Drew moved around and tried to get comfortable, but the state of his undress, or partial undress, was making things dig into him in places he didn't like. He'd never had time to even take his things out of his pocket, or his shoes off. He was pleased when she reached for him in her slumber. Standing next to the bed, he toed off his shoes as he unbuttoned his shirt. His pants, undone, fell to the floor.

She was beautiful. Even with her blouse torn and her bra open, she looked good enough to eat. Laying his pants over the chair with his shirt, he was about to slip into bed when he realized she couldn't be any more comfortable than he'd been. With unsteady hands, he undressed the woman he'd just had the most incredible sex in his life with.

She was so limp that he had some problems getting the rest of her shirt off. She kept reaching for him and more than once he had to take deep breaths to regain some control again. The bra was easy now that her shirt was gone, but Drew couldn't resist taking another sip of her plump breast. By the time he had her skirt off he decided to leave her stockings on. They looked delicious on her and besides, he was afraid he'd hurt himself if he tried to remove them himself. His cock was already hard and ready again.

Drew lay down and Quinn immediately rolled over on top of him. Her hands started stroking him again and he couldn't seem to slow her down—not that he was trying all that hard. When she sat up and spread her legs over his hips Drew rolled her to her back.

"Please," she whispered. "Take me again. I want to feel you inside of me, Drew. Please?"

Taking her hands into his, Drew laced her fingers above her and into the bars on the headboard. She was so hot he could feel her wet heat pull at him. With some of the initial need for her sated, he moved down her body. Every time her hands let go of the headboard he would stop what he was doing. As soon as she put them back, he resumed.

"Good girl," he told her. "My turn now. I'm going to taste you and I don't want you to touch me. You distract me from what I want, and I need to taste you."

"Please, Drew. I need you." He nipped at her nipple. Not hard enough to hurt, but just enough to get her attention.

When he nipped at her hip she rocked up to meet his tongue. By the time he settled between her thighs, he wasn't sure this was a good idea. He wanted to taste her, feel her come into his mouth as he fucked her with his tongue, but his cock was begging for release as much as Quinn was for him to give her one. Opening her nether lips with his fingers, he flicked her clit with his tongue. She arched up at him, her hips leaving the bed.

Taking her clit into his mouth, he pressed two of his fingers deep into her and feasted. Her first orgasm flooded his mouth with her cream, soaking his fingers. He moved down to drink from her and could taste her and him on his tongue. She was hot and spicy. Drew continued to fuck her with his tongue and fingers until she came again, then again. While her body was still trembling from her release, he sat up on his knees and lifted her up and onto him. His cock touched her womb. Taking her breast into his mouth, he lifted her up and down on his cock until he could feel his own release coming. Laying her back to the bed, he pounded into her, hard and quick. Covering her mouth with his, he captured her scream as she came again. Drew came with her; her pulling and milking him drained him.

This time, when he collapsed, he had just enough strength to roll off her and cover them up. His last thought before exhausted sleep took him was that Quinn was everything a man could want in a lover.

~~~

Quinn came awake slowly. She stretched a little but was sore; muscles protested even as they felt weighted and relaxed. She started to roll over to the other side of the bed, but there was something in the way. Opening her eyes, she saw a shoulder, a very large shoulder.

"Please be Jazzie. Please be Jazzie," she whispered to herself as she reached out to touch it.

The low, very masculine groan made her jerk her hand back. When the arm at her waist tightened and pulled her close Quinn noticed that she was naked. And he was naked.

Naked in bed with…she just knew it wasn't going to be good. And when he rolled over, eyes still closed, Quinn did the only thing she knew how to do when she was upset. She got mad.

"What do you think you're doing here? Get up." When he didn't move, she smacked him on his back. "Drew…Mr. Miller, I asked you a question. Get up, I sa— oof."

He rolled over on top of her and put her hands above her head with his fingers laced with hers. She watched his mouth as it lowered to hers. So close, so very close. Scared of what they had done, what they might do again, she let her mouth get ahead of her.

"Did you rape me?"

She knew the moment it left her mouth it wasn't true. Drew jerked back as though she'd slapped him. Fury glittered in his eyes, all traces of sleep gone. Then he rolled off her and got up in what seemed to be one continuous movement. He grabbed up his clothes off the chair and went into her bathroom. The slamming of the door made her flinch.

Quinn wasn't sure what to do. She wasn't even sure what had happened between them. Well, she did know, she supposed, but wasn't ready to remember it yet. She tried to remember what had put them in the bed together when Drew came out and sat in the chair and began putting his shoes on.

"Mr. Mil—"

"Quinn...Miss Waite, if you value your life at all you'll not say a word. Not now, maybe not ever." He stood and stared down at her. "Believe it or not, I don't need to rape women for a simple fuck." He turned on his heel and left.

What had she done? Jumping up, she grabbed her robe and went after him. She wasn't sure what she was going to say when she caught up with him, but it was a moot point. As soon as she rounded the stairs to go down she heard the door slam.

Quinn stared at the door for a moment, the tears she hadn't been aware were falling blurred her vision. She dropped to the floor and started sobbing. That was how Jazzie found her.

"Come on, let's get you some coffee." Jazzie half-dragged, half-led her to the kitchen. "It'll look better after some hot coffee. Maybe. I don't know why people say that, it's not the least bit true. I prefer tea."

"I don't know what happened." Quinn looked down at her full cup as she continued. "He was...we were...I don't know."

Jazzie set a plate of donuts between them, a Saturday morning tradition since moving into this house together. Then a cup of hot tea. Jazzie sat down across from her and took a fat, greasy donut and bit into it before speaking.

"Yeah, I wondered how he'd react to you all over him like that. Men usually like to have some say in sex." Quinn looked up at her sister. "You didn't exactly give him time to make any kind of decisions, you know."

"What do you mean? He started it." A terrible memory danced before her eyes. "Didn't he?"

Jazzie laughed. "Hardly. He came in the door practically spitting he was so pissed that you'd hung up on him, he said. Then you leaned in and took a hunk out of his neck. That shut him right up. Then you pushed him against the wall like he was an all day sucker and you had a major sweet tooth." She took another bite before continuing. "Of course, I'd like a sucker like that to make me scream four times in less than two hours."

Snatches of that were coming back with nightmarish clarity. The stairs, Drew trying to get her to slow down, to savor. Her trying to ride him and him taking her into his mouth.

"Ohnoohnoohno. What have I done?" Quinn had accused him of raping her when it had been her. "I was drunk and I have wanted him for so long."

Jazzie laughed again. "Well, you certainly had him. So what was he slamming out of here about? You wouldn't give it to him again? I'd sure give it to him as much as he wanted."

Quinn couldn't think. She'd hurt him. And not only that, she'd raped him. She had to fix this and now. She stood up to call him to beg him to forgive her when she realized something else. Alyssa was going to kill her.

CHAPTER 10

By Sunday afternoon Drew had written and deleted his resignation a dozen times. He'd picked up the phone to quit at least that many more times as well. He'd dial a couple of numbers or pull Alyssa's number up on his cell phone and stop. Alyssa had nothing to do with this. He'd tell her himself. He even thought about calling Cain. But how did a man tell another that he'd just had the most incredible sex of his life with his sister and she thought he'd raped her?

Drew looked at his watch and groaned. Dinner with his grandda was in an hour. He couldn't miss it. They'd been having dinner together on Sunday nights since before his grandma had passed. But he knew if he went over there in his current condition his grandda would see right away something was wrong.

He went to the kitchen to try and think how he could get out of it when his cell phone rang. It was Alyssa. He so didn't want to talk to her just yet. But he also figured if he didn't then she'd just come over.

"There's a problem at the office. Someone just tried to break in. The police are there now. I'm going over."

Drew closed his eyes. "I'll go, you stay home with Cain. I can meet with them—"

"I said I'd go." She sounded stressed. "Drew, I'm going down now with Cain. Stay away from the building until Monday or I'll…I'll fire your ass. The only reason I called is in the event you hear something on the news. All right?"

"Yeah, sure. But if you need me, I'll be at my grandda's. Call me and I can be there in a matter of minutes."

She assured him she'd be fine and then hung up. He was at his grandda's when he remembered that she was going to have dinner with Cain's family tonight too. He wondered if Quinn would say anything.

His grandda, Thomas Miller, worked for the Howards until Nathan Howard, Alyssa's dad, had passed away. The men had been great friends and probably would have remained so had Nathan not had a heart attack and died. Now, Thomas worked for Alyssa. Some days, Drew thought that his grandda loved her more than him.

"Millie is making my favorite for dinner. Chicken pot pie and baked cherry crunch for dessert. I hope you're hungry." Drew was handed a short glass of amber liquid before Grandda continued. "If you hadn't come over I would have had to eat the entire thing by myself."

"You're too skinny anyway." Drew took a sip of the smooth bourbon. He was so lost in his thoughts he nearly missed his grandda laughing. "What on earth do you think is that funny, old man" Drew asked him with a smile. "You making fun of your favorite grandson?"

"You're my only grandson. You tell her you love her yet?" This was one of the reasons he both loved and hated his grandda so much. He was much too astute and blunt.

"Who? You know something I don't? The only woman I tell I love is the one that I'm currently bopping. Not doing much of that right now." And probably wouldn't for a while yet either, he thought.

"Young people have no respect now days." That statement was said with so much venom it made Drew laugh harder. "I'm talking about that young girl that nearly goes cross-eyed when you enter the room. The boss's sister-in-law."

That shut him up quickly. He knew it was probably too late to play like he didn't know what he was talking about, but he had to try. He looked at the man with as much disinterest as he could fake. "Which one? The girl from accounting? She's not really my type, but if what you say is right then—"

"Damn it, Andrew, you know damn good and well I mean Quinn Waite. That girl has it bad for you and you know it. What are you going to do about it?"

Drew got up, refilled his glass, and downed the entire thing. He had his back to his grandda thinking it would be easier to say what he needed to without looking at him. He hated to lie more than anything, especially to his man.

"Quinn…Miss Waite and I have come to an understanding. We've decided that it just wouldn't work out for us. She will stay out of my way and I'll stay away from her. And if you want me to stay for dinner then you won't say another word about it."

He heard his grandda snort, but he didn't say anything. After several minutes Millie came into the room to announce dinner. They were seated at the table before Drew trusted himself to speak.

"There was a break-in at the Howard building just before I came over here. Alyssa wouldn't let me handle it for her. She and Cain were on their way over when she called me. Did you hear anything about it on the news?"

Drew didn't think he was going to answer and was sorry for that. Drew loved his grandda a great deal and didn't want to have him upset with him. When he finally spoke, his voice was soft and a little brittle. Drew wanted to sob.

"I did. Someone had broken one of the larger windows on the second floor. Not too much damage. The police seem to think it was children playing where they shouldn't have been." Millie served the pot pie before he continued. "I don't think so. That second floor window is fairly high and they would have had to have a strong arm to throw something that far up."

Drew thought he might be right. "Did they mention how the glass was broken? I mean, aren't those window panes almost ten feet wide and at least that tall?"

He grunted with his mouth full of the succulent chicken and broth. Drew took his own bite and closed his eyes in ecstasy. The potatoes and carrots were perfectly done and the chicken was as tender and as juicy as anything he'd ever eaten. The white gravy was thick and hot and just spicy enough that he could taste the bits of herbs used to make it. The crust was so flaky it was like eating slivers of crusty bread dipped in the broth. It was several minutes before either of them even bothered with the homemade bread sliced and steaming sitting in the middle of the table or even looked at the salad that was supposed to accompany the pie.

"Damn, this is the best dinner. I wonder if there's a recipe, or do you think that she has been making it for so long that she knows it by heart?" Grandda took another bite full before going on. "I tell you, son, I could make a mint off this stuff and once she throws in her homemade bread…well, there won't be a plate in the world without at least one or the other on it."

Drew agreed. He took several more bites before he finally took a large bite of salad. This, too, was a work of art. Fresh greens with small, cut up vegetables, salad dressing that was made by the cook and not purchased from a store. Croutons that were still slightly warm and toasty sat on top with bits of fresh mozzarella too.

It wasn't until they were served their cherry crunch that his grandda brought up Quinn again. Drew felt so bad that he told him what had happened between the two of them, well, most of it anyway. He wasn't sure why, but he supposed it was because he needed to tell someone.

"She all right then? Poor girl." He shook his head. "You ever meet her ex-husband? What was his name…Wicket, Carl Wicket. Heard tell he was one sorry son-of-a-bitch. Hit her too."

Drew had heard that too. "How long were they married?"

"I would say about two, maybe three years. That other girl, Sydney, the one in the Special Forces, she came home on leave and took Quinn to the gym and taught her how to fight. I'm pretty sure it wasn't clean fighting either." Grandda cackled. "Heard tell that boy lit out of town when he could move again after she took him on, a few days after he was released from the hospital."

Drew laughed. He could see her too, all up in someone's face giving them what-for. He leaned back in his chair, too full to think about moving. "You didn't ask me if I did what she'd said. Why?" He was touched by the shocked look on Grandda's face.

"Because I know I didn't raise you to hurt a woman. She's had a hard life. You want her, you're going to have to help her get over that part of her life. She is more than worth it, if you ask me."

Drew played with his melting ice cream on his plate and didn't look up when he answered. "I don't. Want her, I mean. I know what you say is true. She has a lot of…hurt, I guess, but I want no part of it. No part of any woman for that matter. I'm not getting married, Grandda. I told you that before."

"Son, you know you don't mean that. She's in love with you and if I'm not mistaken, you're in love with her. Drew, don't—"

Drew's cell phone ringing saved him from having to lie to his grandda about his feelings for Quinn. He was in love with her, but there was no way he was going to marry her. Not anyone for that matter. He was happy to see the ID was Alyssa. He'd even take her knowing what happened between him and Quinn right now over having this conversation with Grandda.

"We're back home now. Everything is fine. But...but the building has been trashed. Whoever got in managed to ransack the place pretty good before the police arrived."

~~~

Quinn looked at what was once her office. It was a mess. Her computer was in several pieces on the floor and all the keys on her keyboard were strewn all over the room. Filing cabinets had been turned over on their sides and though they couldn't be opened, they had done a great deal of damage to the outside of them. Even her chair, her favorite chair, hadn't been spared. There were slash marks all over it and the stuffing pulled out, and it too all over the room. Quinn sat down on one of the turned over cabinets and looked around. It wasn't until she spoke that she realized Alyssa was there.

"It's just stuff. Nothing here that can't be replaced." She came over and sat next to her on the cabinet. "I've already had you set up in another office on the upper floors near mine. All you need to do is go and pick out some furniture for it."

Quinn didn't want new furniture. She wanted this furniture. She leaned over and picked up a broken plant and tried to push in back in the dirt. It wasn't salvageable so she tossed it back down.

"Do you know who did it yet?" She had seen the other offices and hers wasn't even the worst of the mess currently being cleaned up.

"No. The police said kids, but I don't think so. I don't want to brag, but I'm not sure that the 'kids' in this area would do this to us. I have some of my friends asking around. If any of them know anything I'll know it soon enough."

Alyssa had spent ten years living on the streets until just recently. She had been hiding from her mother and uncle at the time. And she was right, if any one of the homeless people knew then they would tell Alyssa in a heartbeat. They loved her very much. Then there were all the things she'd done for them as well.

"I guess I should get to the store. I don't suppose you'd like to come with me, would you?" Quinn looked over at the door before she answered and noticed the big man standing there.

"I'm afraid he'll have to come with us. Cain has decided I need a bodyguard until this is settled. That's Franz Kennedy. He's on duty until noon and then someone else takes over." Alyssa didn't look happy about it, but Quinn knew that she was touched that Cain cared.

They were riding over to the office store when Quinn thought about Drew. She'd not seen him all morning and wondered about that. She thought he'd come by at least once to make sure…she wasn't sure what he'd make sure of, but she hoped he'd come by. She had something to say to him. She had all her notes in her bag and had rehearsed them several times so that she could say it just right. There were eight pages. She hoped he'd let her get at least halfway finished before he walked away. Somehow, she doubted she'd get the first sentence out before he left her. Quinn realized she'd missed something from Alyssa when she laughed.

"Where were you just now? I even started telling you about the incredible sex Cain and I had last night and you didn't bat an eye. I had the same problem with Drew before he left this morning too."

"Left? Where did he go?" Quinn knew she'd made a mistake in asking the moment Alyssa lifted her brow. "I was just wondering with all that's going on why he's not here trying to make sure you don't get into any trouble with the insurance company or something."

Alyssa didn't say anything for so long Quinn fidgeted on the seat. She normally didn't squirm, but Alyssa was making her nervous.

"He was. Here, I mean. But something came up in one of the offices in Paris and he went to oversee it. He should be back sometime next week or the week after. Why?"

The car door was being opened and Alyssa handed out seconds later. Quinn hoped it would give her enough time to come up with an answer. She wasn't sure what to say even after having to pretend to forget her purse and go back inside the plush car and get it. She was hoping Alyssa would forget the whole thing once they got inside the store, but no such luck. As soon as the clerk left them alone, Alyssa asked her again.

"I just thought as your lawyer he'd need to make the claims for the insurance, that's all. What happened in Paris?"

"There were some issues with one of the hotels. Some talk about them going on strike." Alyssa put her hand on her arm and looked at her. '"Quinn, tell me what's going on. Please? You're my friend."

Quinn looked at the desk in front of her and came to a decision. She couldn't hide from Alyssa and she knew it. So she decided to give her half of the truth. Soon it would be time to take action, but not today.

"Nothing. We just had another fight. You know how we are always at one another's throats." She turned away to hide the hurt. "I like this one. And I think I like that credenza over there too."

Alyssa looked as if she wanted to say more, but didn't. Quinn was relieved when the salesclerk came back and helped them with their purchases. It was a long day, but Quinn knew she'd made the right decision in not telling her. She knew that she'd hurt Alyssa, but she also knew that she would forgive her.

CHAPTER 11

Shannon was on hold. As much as she hated making an appointment, she needed to get in to see her daughter. She looked down at her list of things she needed Alyssa to take care of while the hold music droned in her ear. She'd been on hold for nearly ten minutes already.

She'd tried to get in to see Alyssa again two weeks ago, but with all the camera crews and police there she decided to wait. She'd had to purchase a paper to find out what was going on. Someone had tried to break in. The paper had said that it had made a mistake in the reporting of the incident and it wasn't kids breaking in and they now had been told it was vandalism from a group of people. The paper said the police were investigating information given to them by an outside source.

The first person Shannon thought of was Guinevere. She said she was going to make them pay and Shannon thought it was just the kind of white trash thing she'd do. Hire thugs to break into a building and wreak havoc. All she'd managed to do was tighten security and to make

Shannon's life much more difficult. Shannon wished the woman would just go away and leave them all alone.

"Hello, Mrs. Howard? I'm sorry you had to be on hold for so long. The service said that you wanted to make an appointment to see Mrs. Waite. Can you tell me what this is regarding?"

Shannon wanted to scream at her, but knew from past experience all that got her was hung up on and still no appointment.

"Yes. I'm her mother. I'll come in and see her today. This morning would be good for me. I can be there at around eleven." Shannon heard the small laugh, but ignored it.

"Mrs. Howard, I'm afraid I don't have any openings for today. The next appointment I have open is...let me see." Shannon could hear the clicking of nails on a keyboard. "The next appointment I have open for her is on Monday, September twenty-second."

Shannon looked over at the calendar on her desk. It was June tenth. Three months, she expected her to wait three months to see her own daughter? Oh no, that wasn't going to fly.

"I'm afraid that simply won't do. I need to talk to her now. You will need to bump someone and put me into their slot for today. I refuse to wait over three months to come in and have a very important conversation with my own daughter." Shannon's temper was on the edge and it took all she had to reel it in. "I would request that you contact Alyssa and tell her that I need to see her immediately. Tell her...tell her that it's a matter of life or death."

With a "hold please," Shannon was back to listening to elevator music. She knew she had lost it, and took several deep breaths to try and regain control of her temper. The nerve of that girl, her own daughter, treating her as if she was less than what she was when she'd hired and fired her kind daily when she'd been in charge.

She should have known all along that her husband had loved his precious daughter more than he did her. Shannon didn't think having affairs like she had should have had any bearing on her part of his estate. And what on earth had he expected her to do, wait around for him to be there for her? It was entirely his fault that she'd had to turn to others for sex. And then to be reduced to begging for money was beyond cruel. If Nathan were still alive she'd murder him herself for the way she was—

"Mother. What do you want? I don't have the time or the patience for your theatrics today."

Shannon was so stunned by the venom in her daughter's voice that it took her several seconds to remember what she had called for. Shannon picked up her list with shaky hands. "I would like to come and see you about more money. I simply can't—"

"No." Alyssa cut her off. "Now if there isn't anything else, I have things to do. Oh, and don't call in here again and demand anything of my employees. Especially never say that it's a matter of life or death unless it actually is. We both know that you think everything is when it concerns you. If you do, I will simply have your phone shut off. Do I make myself clear?"

"Alyssa, you can't expect me to make appointments to see my own daughter when you let every piece of trash off the streets come in to see you. I'm not going to stand for this treatment much longer." Shannon stood up as she continued. "You'll start to treat me with the respect I deserve or I will—"

"You'll what?" The pause wasn't long enough for Shannon to form an answer. "You know, I don't care. And as for treating you with any kind of respect? I lost all that for you when you drugged me and decided that you'd let me get knocked up by my own uncle so you could control me. Do not call here again. If you do then it is well within my rights to take whatever generosity I've been giving you away and let you live on the streets were you might have to work for a living."

The phone slammed down so hard that Shannon had to jerk the receiver from her ear. She sat back down with the phone still in her hand. It took her several minutes of listening to the dial tone before she put the handset back into the cradle. Then she picked up the entire thing and threw it against the wall.

How dare she? How dare she treat her as if she was nothing more than an irritant? Shannon began pacing the little office. She wouldn't be treated this way, not by anyone and certainly not by Alyssa. She'd brought the brat into this world and she would get the respect she deserved for all the suffering she'd had to endure to do that and the shit she'd put up with since she'd come back to the business. It was time to take action.

Knowing she was going to regret it, Shannon went to the desk again and then had to go to the living room to make a call. Another thing she'd have to purchase on her own because of Alyssa now was a phone. Damn girl was going to pay; Shannon refused to play by Alyssa's rules any longer. She found the number and dialed. When it was answered on the other end, Shannon launched right to it. No point in waiting around any longer.

"Hello, Guinevere. It's Shannon Howard. I'd like to speak to you about what you suggested the other week in the restaurant."

~~~

Quinn started making lists. She was good at making them and better at following them. She'd learned from her ex-husband to do that. He would leave her a list of things to do before he left for work and she'd be expected to have them done plus the daily things before he returned. If she didn't, then hell would have to be paid. He'd beaten her until she couldn't stand, then he'd still expect her to finish the things he'd told her to do anyway. It had taught her a habit that she couldn't break no matter how hard she tried.

The first list was to find a replacement for Alyssa's secretary. She put on this one all the qualifications that the new person would be required to do. On the list was the willingness to shoot first and ask questions later if someone, anyone, tried to harm her. There were other things there as well, but that was the most important.

Her next list was of things she had to do to leave. She'd already been hoarding cash. Sin had told her that she should always have a mode of escape. A car no one knew about, cash and lots of it, and also another identity. The false ID had cost a fortune, but had been well worth it. Quinn had been making "deposits" into her black bag for years, long before Carl had left her, and since working for Howard Corporation, she'd been able to put away a great deal more than she'd hoped for. She knew right to the last penny how much she had and knew it was going to finally be put to good use.

Quinn didn't want to disappear, not really. But she did want to be on her own for a while. She loved her family very much, but knew they'd never understand if she told them she needed some time alone. She looked down at her third list and started to cry.

This was not so much a list as it was a letter in the making. She wanted to apologize to Drew and making a list of things she'd done wrong, things she'd said to him, seemed important in that she needed to make sure he didn't hate her forever. She figured she had two weeks to get it finished. More if he stayed where he was for a bit longer than the two weeks he'd already been gone.

When someone knocked at her door a few minutes later Quinn slipped the lists under the blotter and told them to come in. She wasn't surprised to see Alyssa come in.

"I don't know why you can't just stay my secretary and be done with it. That last woman was an idiot." She went to the little refrigerator, pulled out a bottle of water, and tested it before opening it. "I think that one was really a man dressed up as a woman just to get a job."

"No, she wasn't. She's a retired FBI agent and she is really good at the job. Her last employer said she had saved his ass twice in the ten years she worked for him." Quinn waited until Alyssa took a drink and sat down before she continued. "Your next appointment is in an hour. This one is a man so if he comes in with a dress on, don't say anything."

"Will he? Good heavens, Quinn, where do you get these people?"

"No, I'm trying to make a joke. His name is Clarence Keller. He's been working for different charities for about ten years and has recently decided to…" She realized she was talking to herself. "Alyssa, are you listening to me?"

Alyssa had her phone out and was looking at it oddly. Quinn looked down at her own phone and wondered when the last time was that anyone had called her on it, and then tried to remember if Jazzie had told her if she'd paid the bill or not. Taking out a sheet of notepaper, Quinn started another list marked "bills" and put phone at the top of the list.

"That was Drew," Alyssa said with a heavy sigh. "He just texted me that things are not going as well as he'd hoped and he may be in Paris for another two weeks at the very least. He said that talks are not going well and that he may need to bring over some employees from other hotels to run the Howard until he could get things worked out." Alyssa looked worried. "Do you think I should go over and see if I can help?"

"I don't know, Alyssa. What does Cain say? I'm sure that Dre…Mr. Miller can handle it." Quinn decided to ignore the strange look from her sister-in-law. "I have other appointments for you today, but if you want, I can interview potential people and then send to you the choices I make."

Alyssa stood. "No, you just hire someone. I'm sure if you like them, I will. I have to go and call Cain. He has this thing going at work and I want to be there for him." Alyssa was nearly to the door when she turned back to her. "Quinn, I'm still here if you need me."

Quinn nodded. She didn't trust herself to speak right now. When Alyssa left the office a minute later Quinn laid her head on her desk and cried. She'd been doing that a lot since Drew had left.

Two weeks and not a word. She didn't know what to say to him if he called, but she had missed fighting with him. She missed...well, she missed him. Quinn sat up. She had two more weeks at the minimum and she needed to get going. She pulled out her lists again and started making phone calls.

"Yes, this is Quinn Waite. I need to make an appointment with Mr. Carmichael. I have some things I'd like to change in my will and I need to do so as soon as possible."

"Yes, Miss. Mr. Carmichael is available tomorrow if you can be here at nine in the morning. He has an hour. Do you currently have an attorney or are you looking for something else?"

She wanted to tell the woman that her attorney was in Paris and that she was too in love with him to ask for his help. Oh, and then there was the fact that she'd accused him of raping her, so she was pretty sure he'd not want to represent her in this. Unless her demise was something he wanted, maybe she could get him to make her final arrangements...well, final.

"No. I have—had one, but he's no longer able to help me. I've made some changes in my life and want to make sure things are complete."

"Of course. We understand."

Quinn wanted to cry again, but held on. She made the appointment for tomorrow then set about making her list complete for the next phase of her leaving. Her letter of registration was already typed up and she had set up the payment plan for Jazzie in getting bills paid on time. Her phone had been shut off, but was back on within ten minutes after she'd called in a payment. She was showing the next potential employee a seat when she remembered her physical for her insurance that the company provided. Making a note, she interviewed Mr. Keller.

Four hours and three interviews later, Quinn was exhausted and ready for a hot bath and a glass of tea. She finally had someone she thought that Alyssa would like in Mr. Keller, the first man she'd interviewed. He'd been both personable and very funny. He'd even asked her out, which she'd declined. She was cleaning up her desk when her phone rang. Groaning, she answered.

"I don't have time, nor the energy to talk to you, Mother. State your business so that I can say no and move on." She wished everyday she had the strength to just have her number changed and not give it to her, but she couldn't. "I was just going out the door."

"I wanted to talk to Cain, but he's had me barred from his office. Jazzie won't give me her number and I can't find your other sisters to speak to them. I don't like being treated this way by my own children, Quinn Susan." Quinn was hurt that she'd been a last resort, but let it go. "I would like to meet you for dinner. You'll have to pay, of course. Since that woman your brother has attached himself to killed my Roscoe, I have no income."

Quinn had had a shitty day and a really crappy week. She snapped. "First of all, her name is Alyssa and she's his wife, not some woman. And she didn't kill your Roscoe. He killed himself when he kidnapped me and was willing to kill me for money. Secondly, and most importantly, I'm sick and tired of you blaming every one of us for your problems. If Father left you broke, take it up with someone who might give a shit. I no longer do."

For as much as she wanted to slam the phone down, she gently laid it in the cradle. She sat back down at her desk and burst into tears. She was so sick of her mother and her ways. After ten minutes of feeling sorry for herself, she got up and closed down her office. It was Friday evening and she was going home to a nice comfy bed and her lists. Fuck 'em all.

CHAPTER 12

His plane was late. Drew hated commercial flying, but if he wanted to surprise his grandda on his birthday then he had to do it this way. He paced the lobby once again and then stopped when the little girl sitting next to him started crying. He guessed he should stop frowning too.

He pulled out his phone for the hundredth time and looked at the number there. He'd had her number there for the five weeks he'd been gone, ready to dial, and he'd yet to do it. He put it back in his pocket.

Grandda had been no help at all when it came to getting information about Quinn. He seemed to think she was working too hard, which was more than likely true. And that she was seeing someone. Drew wasn't all that happy about that, but with being out of the country for all this time, there wasn't a whole lot he could do about it. But he was back now and he did plan to say plenty to Miss Quinn Waite.

His flight was called and he had only just sat down when his cell went off. He smiled when he saw who it was. He and Alyssa had planned this for an entire week and she was probably getting antsy because he was late.

"You were supposed to land here over an hour ago. You know I hate this waiting crap. Where are you now anyway?"

"I'm sitting on the plane now. We should be there in an hour. Why do they route you to Chicago then back to Columbus for anyway? Wouldn't it be quicker to just go directly to Ohio?" He grinned when she growled at him. "Alyssa, are you frustrated with me?"

"You know damn good and well I am. I want to be with Cain. He's with Todd Whip tonight and I want that to go well for him and that kid." She took a deep breath and he heard her let it out slowly, blowing off steam he was sure. "Do you know that she told Cain when she made the appointment at the clinic that she was coming in for a checkup? What on earth could she be up to?"

Drew had heard about the woman from Alyssa all week. When Todd had suggested that this woman see a doctor to make sure she was all right, she'd made the appointment the next day. Cain and Cait were going to get her to confess. Drew didn't like this, but he knew that with Cait in charge of the thing Cain would be well protected. He would, however, love to see Cait dressed up as a nurse. That was one beautiful woman.

"She wants her hubby dead and she thinks that Todd is just stupid enough to do it for her." He looked over at the man who was sitting next to him and whispered, 'television show' before he continued with Alyssa. "I have to get off here now. The cell phone sign is flashing. I'll be there soon."

"You'd better be. I'm sick of sitting here waiting. And this new bodyguard smells like dirty shoes."

Drew was laughing when he turned his phone to plane mode. By the time he landed, he'd had four messages from her. Alyssa had wanted to keep him updated and she had. The first message said that Todd had brought the woman to the clinic and was waiting in the lobby for her. Things were going well and that Cait had opted for a pants suit, not a dress. Drew was disappointed, but smiled. Her second message said that the woman wasn't pregnant and had had her tubes tied so there was a very slim chance that she could ever be. Cain had had to leave the room to regain control of his temper at that and Alyssa was sure that he wanted to strangle the woman. The third message said that Todd had played his part well when he'd come into the office and that he'd acted the part of the stupid boyfriend perfectly. He had asked her why she'd lied and she had told him she didn't know what he was talking about. The fourth message had been a little scary, but Cait had handled it well. The husband of the woman had shown up and he was waving a gun around.

"I guess she'd done this sort of thing before and Todd was just the icing on the cake for him. He told her that he was leaving her and when Cait explained that Todd had come to them because his wife had wanted him to kill her husband, he'd fired at his wife. Cain said it wasn't that bad, but he's going to jail and is pressing charges against his wife. What a mess."

Drew agreed. When she came toward him all smiling, he had to laugh. There was a bodyguard on both sides of her and one he could see about three feet behind.

"Are you running for president now? What's with the bookends?" She growled at him again. "Ah baby, you know that he loves you."

"Yes, he does, but doesn't mean I'm not going to shoot him." She started to take his case and the man standing to her left took it from her. "You know, I'm quite capable of lifting...never mind. Let's get you home, Drew."

As soon as they were in the limo Alyssa told him about Quinn. Or she hinted about her. Apparently, she'd never mentioned that he and she had slept together, nor had she mentioned that he'd raped her. He was still mad about that, but that was between Quinn and him.

"She hired me someone to work the office. Clarence Keller. I like him even if he is a bit stiff. I mean, he does laugh, but he isn't Quinn. She's been putting together some killer ideas that are going to make my job easier."

He didn't really care about that, but he asked anyway. "Like what? Dogs in the lobby, or do we now have an x-ray machine and body cavity search going on?"

When Alyssa frowned at him he felt bad. He hadn't meant to sound so snarky, but he knew that he had. He took her hand into his. "I'm sorry. Jet lag, I guess. Tell me what she's been up to. I promise that—"

The limo began to spin around and he was thrown against her. He had just enough time to look out the window and see the truck coming at them from the left. He covered Alyssa with his body just before impact and heard and felt it like he'd been right in front of it. When the car started to roll, Drew grabbed her and held on. Ass overhead, they went tumbling over and over until they came to an abrupt halt on their sides.

He looked down at Alyssa when he was sure they weren't going to roll over and saw the blood on her head. She was looking up at him, but didn't speak. He was scared for her.

"Are you all right?" She nodded. "I'm going to see if I can get up and out, stay here. Call the police."

Drew moved and that's when he heard the voices from outside the vehicle. Someone was shouting at them. Drew put his finger to his mouth to have Alyssa be quiet and started for the door above him. He could see that the driver wasn't moving and hoped that he wasn't dead, but felt the way he was laying there left very little doubt that he was.

"I said come out if you ain't dead. All I want is the girl, whoever else is in there can just stay where you are." Drew looked down at Alyssa when she snorted.

"Like I'm really going to do that," she whispered to Drew. He had to smile; even with a couple of tons of metal wrapped around them, she still had a smart mouth.

Drew thought about their options and decided that they were in the city and that even through the broken glass he could see people starting to come closer to the accident.

"We've called the police and they're on their way. I don't know what you think you might gain from this, but the driver is dead and you are now a murderer. I would suggest that you—"

A spray of bullets hit the limo. Drew could hear them pinging off the metal and he watched as the people he'd seen earlier run for cover. Thankfully, it sounded like the shooter had fired at the undercarriage of the limo or he might have hit one or both of them. Then the silence was broken off by the sound of sirens.

"Christ!" Alyssa said, and he looked down. "You've been hit."

Drew looked at his arm where she had pointed and saw the blood. There was no pain, but he did watch the bright red liquid stain his shirt. His last thought before he passed out was his grandda was getting a hell of a birthday surprise.

~~~

Quinn rushed inside the hospital. She and Jazzie had flown across town and she couldn't remember a single thing about the trip. All Cain had said was that Alyssa had been in an accident and that someone had shot at her. A nurse had met them at the desk.

"She's fine. Come on back and I'll show you. Doctor Waite is with her now and she's fussing up a storm back there. That man that was with her is in surgery and she is fit to be tied that she can't see him." Quinn barely registered what she was saying. "Come on now. Hold up there, girl."

Quinn felt dizzy all of a sudden. She reached for the wall and it shifted away and she fell toward it. Before she could try again she was sitting in a wheelchair and her head was between her knees. She could see feet and knew that it was Cain for some reason.

"Take deep breaths. What did you say to her?" Cain snapped at someone. "Come on, Quinny, you can do it, take deep breaths."

"Let me up, you ass, I'm fine. Cain! Let me up." When he continued to hold her down she kicked out at his shin and he finally let go.

"What happened to you? Did you skip lunch again? Damn it, Quinny, I swear you need a keeper." He moved over to where the nurse was standing and said something low to her and then came back. "I'm running some tests on you and before you object, might I remind you that I hold all the cards right now and that without my okay on your insurance, you are out of work?"

She glared at him. "I hate you right now. And I'm fine. I don't know why you think you have to be the one in charge all the time."

"Because I'm older and hold a medical degree. You'll just give her a little blood and I'll feel better about it."

"Three minutes older, you moronic jackass." She glared harder when he laughed. "Where's Alyssa? I would rather talk to her anyway."

"She's back here. She's fine, I promise. And if it makes you feel any better, I've made them take blood from her too. Drew is still in surgery."

This time, she did hit the floor.

When she woke up she was on a hospital bed and Alyssa and Jazzie were sitting in the room with her. She didn't see Cain, but she could hear him just beyond talking to someone else. Quinn was looking over at her sleeping sister when Alyssa spoke softly.

"You have a bump on your head, but nothing serious. Drew is out of surgery and is going to be fine. They removed the bullet and he's pissed they won't let him up yet." Quinn closed her eyes as Alyssa continued. "Why didn't you tell us?"

Quinn looked at her. "Tell you? I don't know what you mean." She started to sit up, but another wave of dizziness swamped her and she had to rest. She was just starting to slide off the bed when Cain was suddenly there.

"I don't think so. Get your ass back in that bed right now. You have some explaining to do and I'm not letting you out of here until you do. Who is it? Who is the bastard so I can kill him?"

Quinn looked over at Alyssa and the now awake Jazzie. Jazzie colored a bright red and then slipped out of the room. She looked up at Cain. He was furious. She didn't know what was going on, but whatever it was, he was pissed about it. It wasn't until Alyssa spoke again that he stopped glaring at her.

"I don't think she knows, Cain." If Alyssa thought that would help, she was wrong. Cain grabbed her by the arms and shook her. Quinn's teeth rattled.

"You don't know who the father of your baby is?" He shook her again. "What the hell have you been up to that you don't have a clue who fathered your child?"

The next thing she knew Cain was on the floor and Drew was standing over him. He was dressed in a gown and there was a sling on his arm. He looked a bit pale, but Quinn thought he was the most beautiful thing she'd ever seen. Before she could move, he turned to her...or on her.

"Stay right there." Then he turned to Alyssa. "Could you please keep him out of here? I'd like a few words with my...the mother of my child."

Quinn looked over and saw Jazzie standing in the doorway. She knew then that she'd told Drew about the… Quinn looked down at her belly. Could she really be pregnant? She tried to remember when her last period was and couldn't. She looked up at Drew when she heard the door shut.

"Were you planning on telling me? Or was it your plan to hold that over my head along with the rape charges?"

CHAPTER 13

Cain paced the hall. He didn't know if he was pissed at Drew for knocking him on his ass and getting his sister pregnant, or happy because he'd knocked him on his ass and gotten his sister pregnant. He glared at his wife.

"You can look at me like that all you want, big boy. It doesn't make me the least bit happier with you either. You had no right to treat your sister that way." She sat down on the plastic chair. "And you can forget any kind of 'woo hoo, I'm alive' sex now. I'm pissed at you too."

He sat down next to her, picked her up, and put her onto his lap. "I'm sorry. It was so…I didn't expect her to be pregnant. And Drew? Damn, he has a quick left."

She kissed his cheek. "You should have seen his face. I don't think I've ever seen him that pissed off before. What do you think he's saying to her?"

"If he knows what's good for him, he's telling her they're getting married. Then he's telling her he loves her." Cain looked at his wife. "He does, doesn't he, love her I mean?"

Alyssa leaned her head on his shoulder. "If you had asked me that before this, I would have said yes. But now...I don't know. She never told me they'd gone that far. And she seemed just as surprised as you and I did."

"She loves him," Jazzie said as she came up and sat next to them. "The night that he came over...I thought she might be pregnant a couple of days ago and never said anything. I told Drew what was going on. I think...I think Quinn is going to be mad at me over this."

Cain pulled Jazzie closer to him. "Nah, she won't. Once they figure out this thing, you'll see, they'll be so happy that they're having a baby they won't remember any of this."

At least he hoped so. He wished he could go in there and find out, but knew that he couldn't. Quinn was a grown woman. He looked down at Alyssa. Drew had saved her for him because he had no doubt that she was the woman that the idiot shooter had been trying to get to. He pulled her closer into his arms. He couldn't live without her and wondered who the mad man was now that was trying to take her from him.

They sat there for another twenty minutes before the police came down the hall. Cain had tried to put them off, but Cait had told him that she needed answers and the sooner they got them the quicker they could get to the bottom of this.

Cait was coming around the corner when Drew came out of Quinn's room. He didn't look any happier now than he had when he'd gone in. Before he could ask, Drew went down the hall toward where his room had been.

"I would like to speak to you, Alyssa, then I'll go down and talk to Drew. I'm sure you know that the sooner we get out a description, the sooner we can see if we can get this guy. What can you tell me about what happened?" Cait sat down next to them. "I know you said you were inside the vehicle when the guy shot at you, but did you hear anything?"

Cain let Alyssa sit on another chair and he stood up. He didn't know who he wanted to talk to more, Quinn or Drew. He owed them both an apology and he wanted to do it now. He decided to see Drew first. Since he wasn't going to release Quinn he knew she was staying where she was.

Drew wasn't in his bed when he got to his room. Cain could hear him in the bathroom and simply sat down to wait. When he came out, Cain was surprised to see him dressed.

"Going somewhere? I was told you would be here for another couple of days at the very least." Cain didn't think he was going to answer him. "Drew, I'm sorry about what happened in Quinny's room. I didn't...I was surprised, that's all."

"She won't speak to me. I tried talking...well, that's not true. I yelled mostly. She just sat there." Drew looked at him then. "The one time I don't want her to shut up and she does."

Cain sat down on the end of the bed. "What are you going to do about the baby? I mean, I'm assuming it's yours."

"It's mine. And I don't know yet. I will be a part of her life and help her raise it, marry her as soon as it can be arranged, but right now I'm trying to deal with just knowing I'm going to be a father." He looked at Cain with a sloppy grin. "I'm going to be a dad."

Cain laughed. "Yeah, if she doesn't kill you first. What are you going to tell your grandda?"

"Holy shit, Grandda. He doesn't know. I mean, of course he doesn't know about the baby, but he doesn't know I'm here. I gotta call him. Shit, it's late." Cain looked at his watch. It was just after two in the morning. "Think I should call him?"

Cain laughed. "I think if you don't, Quinny will be the very least of your worries. I'll leave you alone to call. Cait will be down soon to talk to you anyway. I'm going to go and grovel with my sister. See if I can get her to forgive me."

Alyssa wasn't in the hall when he rounded the corner. He could see the two officers that had come with Cait in the hall outside the waiting area and the closer he got, he could see that both the women were in there. He smiled at the expression on Cait's face. He knew that whatever was going on she wasn't happy about it. Cain knocked on his sister's door and slipped inside.

The room was empty. He sat in the chair and waited for her to come out of the bathroom, assuming that was where she was. He sat there for perhaps five minutes when he realized that he hadn't heard anything. Getting up and just knowing he wasn't going to like it, he knocked on the door.

"Quinn, I want to talk to you. Come on out. I just had a talk with Drew and he and I have mended our differences." Nothing. "I'm sorry, baby. Come out and let's talk." The nurse coming into the room startled him and he turned to look at her. "I think she's still mad at me. Could you please go in and make sure she's all right?"

The nurse nodded and he moved when she came up to the door. She simply took the handle, turned it, and stepped inside. She came back out with a frown. "There's no one in here, Doctor Waite." Cain looked over her shoulder and could see the entire room. "Let me go and see if she was taken for tests."

Cain knew that she hadn't been taken to any tests; he hadn't written any orders for her to have them. He looked around the room and could see that her bag of clothes were gone, as was her purse. He sat down on the bed. Fuck. She was gone.

~~~

Quinn sat in the back of the taxi and closed her eyes. She'd seen Cain coming down the hall toward her room when she'd stepped into the elevator. He even looked right at her. She had never been so scared in her life.

She had the driver take her to the house where she would grab what she could and leave. Quinn knew it was cruel to run out on Alyssa right now, but she had to get away. Especially now. Quinn put her hand over her flat belly and marveled again that there was a child there.

The phone was ringing when she walked into the house. She didn't bother answering it. She knew it had to be one of the three people she was trying to get away from. Cain would be mad because she was pregnant, Alyssa because Quinn hadn't given her notice, and Drew because…well, because. Moving the small panel from the wall in the pantry, she reached in and took out the duffel she'd hidden there.

Quinn opened the bag and took out the envelopes she'd put in there only just last night. While circumstances had changed, her needing to leave and the reasons for it hadn't. She was nearly out the door when she heard Cain's voice over the answering machine.

"Quinn, call me back when you get this. If you're running away because I hurt you, please don't. I'm sorry, sorrier than I've ever been. Please, honey, call me back. I love you."

She closed the door and left.

Getting back into the taxi she'd had wait for her, she asked him to take her to the bus stop. It wasn't where she wanted to go, but she knew that if asked the driver would have to tell them where he'd dropped her. She also knew that she had to purchase a ticket too. But for now she leaned back and cried.

Drew's child. She was going to have his baby and he couldn't stand her. She thought about the conversation they'd had after he'd had her family leave the hospital room.

"Are you all right? Do you need anything?" She shook her head no. "Good. Because you are by far the stupidest woman I've ever met. You've lost weight and you're having my baby. Are you trying to lose it? No, that can't be right because according to your sister you had no idea you were even going to have my child. How is that possible?"

Quinn didn't say anything because she frankly didn't know what to say. She had already figured that Jazzie had told him that she was pregnant, but she didn't know that she also knew about the baby. Before she could wonder why her own sister hadn't told her Drew started in with his plans of marriage.

"As soon as it's possible, we're getting married. And before you open your mouth and say that there isn't going to be one then think again. I won't have my child born as a bastard. And you'll be getting prenatal care as soon as I can arrange it. I'll have to call in a favor or two, but tomorrow I'm going to have someone come here and examine you to make sure you're fine. And you won't be working any more long days either. You'll be working eight straight a day and then home."

She had watched him pace. It might have been funny, cute even, if she wasn't so sure he wasn't just doing this because he thought she was too stupid to do this on her own. Quinn leaned back on the bed and did her own planning.

As he went on about her living arrangements she tried to remember if she'd done everything on her list. When he mentioned that she was going to need to start sleeping longer hours she was working on getting the IV out of her hand. By the time he was standing over her glaring she'd decided that enough was enough. She would not let another man bully her.

"Are you going to say anything or just lay there? You're not helping matters by being stubborn, Quinn." He looked so angry at her. "If this about your accusations about me raping you, we both know what happened that night and it was you who started it. And now we both have to pay for the consequences."

Her heart had broken at that very moment. And she also knew that no matter what her feelings for him had been, he was no different of a bully then her ex-husband had been. The only difference was Carl used his fists and Drew, words.

The bus station was nearly empty when she got there. The cab driver asked her if she was going to be okay and she could tell he knew she'd been crying. But after giving him a generous tip he went on his way. She went to the counter and purchased a ticket for the first ride out using her credit card to do so. A five day trip to California cost her over two hundred dollars.

The trip to the bathroom had her flushing the ticket and cutting up the credit card. She was pretty sure it wouldn't flush so she put some of the little pieces in each of the little trash cans in each of the fourteen stalls. She didn't know if it was necessary, but it made her feel like she was doing something productive. Pulling on the big hat and the ugly coat she'd gotten two summers ago on clearance, she left the bathroom and went to the parking garage on Fifth.

The car had been a good buy when she'd gotten it eight years ago. It was when gas was cheap enough to make driving a gas guzzling machine not quite such an expense. Now with gas at nearly four bucks a gallon, it was going to cost a fortune to drive even across the street. Getting in it, she drove the eight miles to her apartment on Brown Street.

By the time she'd taken her bag inside and taken the cloths off the furniture she was exhausted. But she was also hungry. Ordering from the local Chinese place, she sat down to wait and to get her new cell phone charged.

Quinn knew she couldn't hide out forever. And she had no intentions of doing so now that the baby had come along. But she did need a break. Her plan was to stay here until she could get her head on straight. Now she needed to make plans about the baby too. Pulling out a sheet of paper from her purse, she started writing down her own rules.

No marriage. No matter what Drew said she wasn't going to marry him. She wouldn't marry anyone for all the wrong reasons and just because she was going to have a baby didn't mean she needed to make another mistake and marry. She had to find a job too. Not that she couldn't afford to live off the money she'd saved, but she didn't think she could remain idle. Quinn had been working all her life and didn't see any reason not to continue to do so now.

By the time the delivery boy had shown up she started feeling like she'd taken control of her life again. When she'd eaten the last of the lo mein noodles, she was beginning to believe she'd made the right decision. Going to the bedroom she didn't so much as lie down, but fell into the bed and closed her eyes. For the first time in her adult life and maybe even before Quinn didn't set the alarm and she didn't worry about laying her clothes out for the next day.

CHAPTER 14

Shannon watched the news again. She'd actually done it. Guinevere had hired a man to kidnap Alyssa just like she said she was going to do. Of course it had failed. Miserably failed, but she had done it. Without taking her eyes from the news account she answered the phone without looking at it.

"So, did you see it? That fool Sheppard fucked it all up, but she'll come running back to you now, see if she doesn't." Speak of the devil—Guinevere. "I've already taken care of him so you don't have to worry about that."

Shannon had a second to wonder just how she'd taken care of the man, but they were pulling Alyssa out of the limo again and she wanted to see that. She looked so helpless and every time Shannon saw it she got just a little happier. Yes, by God, this might work.

"I was going to go down to the hospital, but the news report hasn't said which hospital they had taken her to." She called them both, too, and they wouldn't give her any information unless she could provide them with the code to do so. "I don't suppose you know which one, do you?"

"Bethesda. The one on Forrest Avenue. Cain has privileges there and that's where they took them both." They were pulling out the man when Guinevere suddenly spoke up. "Hey, do you know that man she was with? I can't seem to make out his face on this TV I got."

Oh, Shannon knew him all right. The lawyer. "Andrew Miller. His grandfather used to work for my late husband. He's been a pain in my ass since Alyssa came back."

"Hum, nice-looking guy. Wouldn't mind getting a little of that myself." Shannon shuddered at that when Guinevere cackled at her own joke. "He single that you know of?"

"No, I don't know." She started to ask if she thought he might be a tad too young for her, but decided she really didn't care all that much to know. "So, what do we do now? You said this was a three part plan."

"Next, we go after one of mine. That way there's no suspicions about you or me having anything to do with this. I was thinking that we'd go after Quinn. She's the one that had my Roscoe killed, you know."

Shannon didn't know her version of the events, but the paper had said that he'd taken his own daughter and had held her for ransom for the two million dollars that he felt had been promised him. Shannon honestly thought that Alyssa should have paid him. She had no idea why her daughter had to be so tight-fisted with her money. It wasn't as if she didn't have plenty.

"You know what you're supposed to do, right? You snatch her right from her office and then take her to that place that idiot was supposed to take your kid." Guinevere snorted. "Watch out for the mess in there. I don't think the people who helped me with my…let's call it a problem, were all that neat."

Shannon hung up and wondered again what she was doing with such a lowlife as Guinevere. Shannon didn't mind Cain so much, not now that she knew he was a doctor. She loved telling her friends that her daughter had married a doctor. She smiled when she said it. She was sure all her friends were jealous that her daughter had done so well for herself. Shannon frowned when she thought about how few of her friends had been around lately and blamed that on Alyssa as well.

"Ungrateful kid. Just like her father." Shannon went to the liquor cabinet and took down the cheap bourbon that she'd been reduced to buying. "That's her fault too."

Shannon was well into her fourth bourbon when Samuel came in with her son Robert. She looked at the two men and wondered what the hell she'd done to deserve such assholes as relatives. Then she giggled. Oh yeah, she'd fucked one and birthed the other.

"Mother, must you? You're as bad as Colleen with her cheap liquor. That's one of the reasons I divorced the stupid twit. If you must drink," her son said with a condescending tone, "please do so behind the closed door of your room. I so do not want to see you like this. It's unbecoming of a Howard."

Shannon laughed harder. "You do know that the only reason you're a Howard is because I was married to one at the time I conceived you, don't you? I'm not even sure who your father is come to think of it."

"Really, Shannon, get up. There is no reason for you to rehash all that now. We have news about Alyssa. Did you know that she'd been in an accident today? I don't suppose it's too much to hope that she was killed?" Shannon looked over at her lover and brother-in-law. "Oh don't look at me like that. You know as well as I do that you wish the chit was dead."

Shannon supposed she did, but there was no reason for someone to point it out to her. Alyssa had been a pain in her butt for longer than she'd care to think. And her being married now just added insult to injury. If she managed to get herself pregnant too, then that would make Shannon a grandmother and she did not want that to become a reality.

"No, she wasn't hurt. But the idiot who was supposed to do the job is." Shannon giggled again. "I've been told it was messy. Messy, messy, messy."

Robert glared at her while Samuel left the room. She'd had about enough of all of them. She had no men in her life that gave her any respect, she thought. Hell, even her own daughter treated her poorly.

"Oh by the way," Robert started. "I'm going to need to have more money soon. I got this girl preggers, or so she claims. But you'll have that." He flopped down in the chair across from her.

Shannon just looked at him. He couldn't possibly be serious. There was no way that he expected her to...

"So how much do you suppose she should get, Robert? One hundred, two maybe?" Shannon sat up more on the couch. "It doesn't matter. We don't have that kind of money no matter what the amount is."

Robert snorted. "I doubt a hundred bucks will buy her off anyway. I have no idea how much it'll cost and frankly, I could care less. Just pay it."

Shannon stood up and over her son. "Did you not hear me? There is no money to pay her off. You'll have to...I don't know, work something out with her or something."

Robert stood up so quickly that Shannon nearly fell back. She was suddenly afraid of him. When he doubled his fist up she was sure he was going to hit her.

"Get the fucking money. I don't care where, but you pay this bitch off. Go to that bitch of a daughter of yours. She's certainly got it."

Cowering now, she looked up at her son. "She won't...she refuses to see me. She said that she doesn't have to—"

The slap made her fall. She was on the floor and looking up at him as he towered over her. She wondered how he'd gotten so tall, so large, and knew without a doubt that he would hurt her more if he wanted to.

"Tell your daughter," he said between clenched teeth, "that if she doesn't pay her off then she will get more of what I just gave you. Do you understand me?" Shannon nodded. "Good. Now I'm going out and if you know what's good for you, you'll shut the fuck up and do what I tell you."

Shannon stayed on the floor until she heard the front door open and then slam closed. She crawled her way to the phone and called the only person she knew who could help her. "Guinevere, do you know of someone I can hire to hurt someone?"

~~~

Drew was sitting on the couch at his grandda's feeling sorry for himself when Millie brought him his lunch. His arm hurt, but not all that badly. He was just trying to figure out how to eat the sandwich when she took it from him and started cutting it up. He knew she was pissed. First, because of the way she sawed at his food; second, because she was sawing at his sandwich. She'd been in the room three times in the last hour and huffed at him every time. He just didn't know why yet. The way she was cutting up his meal he had a thought that she was visualizing some other part of his anatomy.

"Millie, I—"

"Shame on you, Andrew Miller. Shame, shame. If your mother was here she'd...she'd beat you with a wet noodle. I have never...what did you...damn it." She tossed the knife and fork on the plate and stood. "What did you expect that poor girl to do? Just let you tell her what she was to do? Shame on you."

He wasn't sure if he should answer and decided that maybe he should try and defend himself just a little. "She wasn't going to tell me about the bab—"

"And when did you expect her to tell you? While you was in Paris? Or maybe while she was lying flat on the floor?" He had a moment to wonder how she had so much information, but she answered that too. "My sister is a nurse there and she told me that the poor little thing just found out herself. That you even told her yourself she was having your child."

"Millie, I was upset. I'd just had to hit her brother for shaki—"

"Oh yeah, you're quick to jump to her defense when someone else hurts her, but not when you open that trap of yours to hurt her." She was pacing now, striding back and forth in front of him like she was on a mission. "And now she's run away from you. Imagine that! What are you going to do about this, I ask you? How are you going to make it so that I will hold that precious babe?"

Drew was getting madder by the minute. Yes, he'd known this woman all his life and she'd paddled his butt on more than one occasion when he'd stayed with his grandparents, but this was too far. "You don't know what you're talking about. She came on to me, not me to her. She got pregnant because she was not willing to tell me if it was safe. A man can only do so much when a woman is all over him."

She stopped pacing and stared at him. He could see the disappointment in her eyes and a bit of shock. When she turned and walked away he started to stand to go after her, but she stopped suddenly and turned back.

"You were taught to keep it in your pants if you don't have protection, were you not?"

"Yes, ma'am." If the subject matter wasn't so adult, he'd swear he'd just stolen a cookie from the jar.

"And were you not also taught that you are just as responsible for what your body does to someone else as the person you are doing it to?" she asked him softly.

"Yes, ma'am." He'd been taught that one from her when he'd hit Billy Wade down the street. That hadn't hurt as bad as this dressing down did.

"And were you also taught that men and women were equal in all things? Including sex, fighting, and even jobs?"

"Yes, ma'am, I was."

She nodded at him. "Then why are you blaming only her for your child being in her belly?"

The door closing behind her sounded like she'd slammed it in the quiet of the room. He turned to his grandda when he heard him clapping. He walked over, sat across from Drew, and simply stared for a few minutes. When he did speak Drew wanted to go find a corner and stand in it.

"Millie has loved you all your life and your grandma used to say she only stayed with us all these years to get to be around you." Grandda sat back in the chair. "You hurt her, son. And that girl. What do you plan to do about either woman?"

He honestly didn't know. He knew that he had to find Quinn or he'd never be able to fix it with her, and without fixing it with Quinn he couldn't fix it with Millie. He'd screwed up, he knew that. And to add more onto it, he'd added insult to injury by hurting her again when he'd seen her in the hospital.

"I don't know. I...I screwed up. I don't know how to fix it. Grandda, what do I do? I want to be a part of their lives. I need to be a part."

Grandda nodded. "Do you love her?"

Drew didn't love her. He liked her well enough. He didn't even mind her all that much when she was at her most irritating, but love her? No, Drew didn't love her. He didn't think.

"I don't know. I know I should say that I do. That I slept with her because she meant the world to me, but love her? No, Grandda, I don't love her. I'm not even sure that most of the time I even like her."

Grandda nodded. "That's what I thought. Then, son, you only have one choice. Leave her alone. Support her financially if she needs it, give her the best care you can provide her, but don't marry her. It would be a monumental mistake on both your parts."

Drew looked at his grandda, confused. "Wait. You're telling me not to marry the woman I got pregnant? You're telling me to basically only be there when she needs me and nothing more?"

"That's right. I'm not saying stay out of the child's life. It's not his fault that you don't love her. I'm just saying that you don't need to compound your...both your mistakes by marrying. Especially if you don't think you love each other." Grandda stood up. "Well, I have a date. You don't stay up too late now. I'll see you in the morning."

Drew sat on the couch and stared at nothing. He was having some difficulty trying to wrap his head around the advice that his grandda had just given him. Don't marry her. His grandda was actually telling him not to marry her.

CHAPTER 15

Quinn took the entire weekend to get her head together. On Sunday night she called her sister Lilliane and talked to her for over an hour. Quinn never mentioned the fight she'd had with Cain or Drew; she didn't mention the baby either. She and Lilliane talked about her new class full of kindergarteners and they talked about visiting.

"You should see it down here. The weather is wonderful and the trees are turning. I love it. I don't think I have had a more wonderful group of kids either. Come down for a while. It'll be fun."

Lilliane Iris, or Lilly to her friends and family, lived in Nashville, Tennessee. She had been a kindergarten teacher since she'd been fresh out of college and had done nothing else. She'd fulfilled her lifelong dream of becoming a teacher. Quinn couldn't be happier for her.

"I'll let you know in a few days. Right now I need to get me a job and I want to move out on my own for a while. Jazzie is great, but..."

"But she can be a bit hard on the nerves. Yeah, been there, done that." Lilly laughed. "All right, let me know. I have a few days sick time coming to me and if you let me know I can take a long weekend with you."

On Monday morning Quinn was ready to face the lion. She called the office to make an appointment with Drew. His secretary answered like she was completely out of her element.

"Oh Miss Quinn, this place is falling apart. Falling apart, I tell you. I've never seen someone...why, if he snaps at me once more, I'm quitting. I will. I don't need this kind of crap."

"Don't quit. Please don't. Just take a deep breath and let it out slowly." Like she could give advice on dealing with Drew, she thought. "Here's what I want you to do. Type up your resignation and the next time he snaps lay it on his desk and then take a long lunch."

"Oh no, I couldn't do that. I need this job. I was only...he isn't so bad. I'll just set you up with an appointment."

"Do you want him to keep snapping at you? If you don't then you'd better take a stand. Give your notice and then if that doesn't work I'll talk to Alyssa for you and we'll get you transferred to another department. You don't have to take that from him."

"You'll stand behind me? Well, he has been a bear. I'll do it. Yes, I will." Quinn could hear the confidence returning to Caroline's voice over the keys clicking. "I have an opening today at one-fifteen. Can you do that one?"

Quinn wanted to get this over with, but did she want to that quickly? Sheesh! "Yes. Yes, that'll be fine. Thank you, Caroline."

"No, Miss Quinn, thank you. Is there anything else I can do for you?"

Yes, Quinn thought, make the last week go away. "No... Yes. Can you transfer me to Alyssa's office, please? I need to make an appointment with her too."

A few seconds of music and Alyssa answered the phone. Quinn waited after she said hello, hoping that she would think the phone went dead or the connection was lost. She should have known better with Alyssa.

"I can hear you breathing. If you hang up I'll never forgive you. I...Quinn, please come home. I miss you." Then the richest woman in the world, one who ran several corporations at once, burst into tears. "Please come in and talk to me. I want to see you, make sure...please?"

Quinn was crying too now. "Damn it, I said I wanted to make an appointment with you, not make you cry. Alyssa, I needed to get away. I had to, you understand? He was...Drew was...and Cain, he...oh, Alyssa."

Both of them were sobbing by now and Quinn promised she'd come in now and see her before she saw Drew. That was going to be hard enough without having swollen eyes, but she'd go. She was pulling into the office about an hour later, just after eight-thirty.

When she came into the building, she was waved by. She didn't stop to tell them she didn't work there anymore, she was too upset, and besides, new people coming in had to have someone come and get them and she just wanted to go up. When she knocked on Alyssa's door she went in and was immediately engulfed into Cain's arms.

"Shut up and let me hold you," he said when she started to struggle. "I'm so sorry. So very sorry, Quinn. I shouldn't have…I was a prick and an ass and I'm so sorry. Please don't leave like that again. I couldn't find you and…well, don't do it again, okay?"

"Cain, I can't breathe." He released her immediately. "I'm sorry too. I shouldn't have left like that, but it was too much."

He hugged her again, only this time it was much gentler. She went around the desk and hugged Alyssa. She would never have considered herself a hugger, but it felt good. Very good. She sat in the chair and held her brother's hand.

"Now what?" he asked her. "You notice I'm not yelling and not telling you what to do. Alyssa pointed out the error of my ways. I need to be supportive and happy for you if you're happy. Are you? Happy, I mean?"

"No, not really. I'm pregnant, I'm unemployed, and I have no home." Quinn looked at Alyssa when she snorted. "Well, I am. I can't…you have to know I can no longer work here. Especially now. I have to—"

"And why not? You've got a job here. I refuse to accept your resignation. You have a home, even if you have to come and live with us. The house is certainly big enough and while I can't do a thing about the pregnancy, I can help you that way. I'm just about eight weeks ahead of you there."

Quinn sat there for several seconds and tried to work out what Alyssa had just said. Eight weeks ahead…ahead of what? When Quinn looked over at Cain it was as if a light went off.

"Christ! You're pregnant too. Oh my God! That's wonderful." Quinn got up again and hugged her sister-in-law. "That's so wonderful. I'm so excited for you."

"Hey! You know I had something to do with it too." Cain laughed. "I'm pretty sure she couldn't have gotten that way on her own."

Quinn went back around and hugged her brother, not even caring that he squeezed her too tight again. She was so happy for them she started crying again. "I'm so happy for you both. I don't know why I keep crying about everything. The kid, I guess. You must think I'm a ninny. Let me go and get cleaned up." She dashed off to the bathroom before either of them could say anything.

A baby. Her brother was going to have a baby. Quinn laid her hand over her own belly. They would be cousins, hers and his. She looked in the mirror and wondered if now would be a good time to tell them what she had decided. No, not today. It would wait until she talked with Drew. After splashing cold water on her face, she went back into the office.

They talked until she was hoarse and felt like she needed a nap. She had wondered how Cain had gotten to the office so quickly and he'd told her he was already there. She flushed slightly when she realized how she'd made Alyssa cry. He said he'd just come over to see her and just happened in the office when she was hanging up.

At one, she made her way to Drew's office. She was armed with her list and her determination. When Caroline told her to go on in as soon as she got there Quinn had a moment of panic, but shoved it down and knocked on the door. When he told her to come in she nearly bolted then, but opened the door and walked in. It was the hardest three steps she'd ever taken.

~~~

Drew knew she was in the building. Had known since the moment she'd pulled in the lot that she was close. He'd had security watching out for her since she'd left him on Wednesday. He had been pacing his office since ten wondering if he should go down to Alyssa's office and drag her back here or wait. He had waited. It hadn't been easy, but he'd done it. He kept thinking about what his mother had told him.

"You can't possibly tell me that you don't love her, Andrew. Why, she's all you've talked about for months."

His grandda had called his parents as soon as he'd found out that Drew had been hurt. They'd shown up not long after his grandda had told him not to marry Quinn. She'd told him basically the same thing. Don't marry her but support the baby.

"I don't. She was just someone I wanted. And I know you find this hard to believe, but I am over twenty-one and I have been making decisions on my own for a while now."

"Don't be arrogant, Andrew. I can still ground you." Wisely, he kept his mouth shut. "All right, if you don't love her then please don't marry her. It's hard enough having a single parent, but it's worse when the parents hate each other."

Drew's mom, Rose Dale Miller, had been raised by her father after her mom had left him for another man.

Drew didn't know his other grandda, he'd died before Drew was born, but he'd always imagined him to be a bitter, cold man.

"What does Dad say about this? Is he fine with me having a bastard son?" Drew had a tone and he knew his mother had heard it too.

"He'll only be a bastard to you, apparently. To me he'll he my grandbaby. And if this is the way you spoke to Quinn then its small wonder she didn't slap you before she left."

Drew didn't know why everyone was taking her side. His entire family was all for him not marrying her and her raising his child on her own. He'd always thought of himself as a "catch," as his grandma used to say. Apparently he was nothing more than pond scum. Now as Quinn stood in front of him, her eyes swollen and her nose red, he felt that way too.

"Quinn. Have a seat."

She sat in one of the chairs about two seconds before she stood up. She slapped her hand over her mouth and dashed to his bathroom. She was inside and the door shut before he could react.

Drew went to the door and started to knock when he heard her retching. He took a step back then another as he heard her crying as well. He turned to his door and went to the reception area.

"Caroline! Come quick. She's sick. I didn't...Christ! She's really sick in there." Panic was rising and he knew he was losing it. But he couldn't seem to stop it.

Caroline stood. "She's just nervous. That's all. Nerves and babies don't mix well." She started moving toward his office slowly, much too slowly, Drew thought. "Why don't you call down to the cafeteria and tell them you need a glass of tea for Quinn and some crackers?"

Drew was so grateful for something to do he snatched the phone up like it was a lifeline and he was about to take his final dip in the ocean. As Caroline stopped long enough to tell him the extension he had a moment of complete clarity. He loved her. Drew was head over heels in love with Quinn Waite.

CHAPTER 16

Robert hung up the phone. He didn't have any idea how the lawyer had gotten his number, but he was going to find out. The nerve of that guy demanding Robert own up to his responsibilities or else. The girl had enjoyed herself, he supposed. If she got pregnant then how was that his fault? Damn it.

Usually, he just had his mom take care of this kind of shit, but since her brat had come back she'd been pretty unreliable. He didn't see why he had to deal with this when he'd never had to before. Picking up the phone again, he dialed his mother.

After getting no answer and refusing to leave her a message to call him back he called his uncle. Uncle Samuel answered on the second ring.

"Where's Mom? She isn't answering her fucking phone and she needs to take care of this issue. I'm not dealing with this crap, it's not my job."

Samuel had been his father figure for a long time. When his...well, Robert wasn't really sure what Nathan

Howard had been to him, but when he'd been too busy with Alyssa, Robert had turned to Samuel. He was the one who'd taught him how to shoot a gun and had taken him to all his martial arts classes.

"I haven't seen her since yesterday. She was supposed to go by and see her daughter, but I'm not sure that panned out either." Samuel snickered as he continued. "The daughter is more like her mother than either of them realize in her stubbornness."

Robert didn't give two shits about Alyssa except in that she'd taken all their money. They'd been just fine after the old man died until she showed up again. Now they were living in this pigsty and tripping over each other all the time. They'd gone from a twenty-bedroom house with maid service, cooks, and all the money he could ever spend to this...hole-in-the-wall with only five bedrooms and a person who only came in to clean once a week. And no one did his laundry or cleaned up his room. And forget cooking. They'd been eating out for the past year and he was sick and tired of it, and the cheap fast food shit.

"Somebody gave that slut's attorney my number and the guy is hounding me for payment. I don't know who gave it to him, but hell is going to be paid when I find out." Not to mention someone was going to pay for his aggravation too. "I need this gone."

"I would assume your sister's attorney gave it to him. They know who used to pay the bills and her lawyer is slick in that he's made it so Alyssa isn't responsible for any of our bills or anything we might incur since she kicked us out." Samuel laughed. "That's why there is no money in the coffers. Your mom is taking care of that as we speak."

While Robert liked the sound of that, he didn't hold out much hope. His mother was an idiot as far as he was concerned. And she wasn't going to stand up to anyone if she didn't have to. He smiled when he thought about her cowering on the floor at his feet.

"Do you know what she's doing? I'm betting whatever it is, she'll fuck it up. Leaving her in charge of anything is bound to fail." Robert went to the television, not able to find the remote, and turned it on. At once, he was pissed again. "The fucking cable is out again. Who am I gonna have to kill to get some fucking service around here?"

Samuel laughed. Robert didn't see what was so funny when his life was going to shit and no one cared. He wanted to throw something or hit someone. Looking around the room, all he could see were a couple of old vases and some pictures. That's when he got the idea to talk to Alyssa himself. Looking at his sister's picture with old man Howard and his mother he thought it was high time he did a little up close and personal time with dear old sis.

"I gotta go, Uncle Samuel. If that asshole lawyer calls again tell him...tell him to fuck off. Robert Howard does not pay for sex."

"Will do. Oh, and Robert."

Robert closed his eyes, knowing he was going to hate whatever his uncle had to say next.

"The cable's off because your mother decided getting her hair done was more important than the cable bill. And don't expect there to be any cable in the near future either."

Robert was almost afraid to ask. "And why's that?"

"Your sister isn't paying for it anymore. Or a great many other things either. She said it's about time we got jobs and started working. Also…" He paused for almost too long, thought Robert. "She said her obligation to us ends in six months according to the will from her dear old dad."

Robert picked up the picture and threw it against the wall. His uncle was laughing harder now and before Robert did something incredibly stupid like piss him off, he hung up the phone.

He started throwing anything he could get his hands on now. Nothing was spared. Books were strewn about the room as pages fluttered to the floor. The two vases that he knew were gifts to his mother from his brother Nathan shattered against the wall. As soon as he put his hands on something, it was destroyed. An hour after hanging up on his uncle, Robert was in his car speeding across town. It was high time he and his sister dear had a long talk.

~~~

Quinn woke up on a couch. It took her a couple of seconds to realize where she was, but when she did she sat up quickly. Then immediately lay back down with a groan.

"Cain said you should try getting up slowly or try eating a few crackers before you sit up. He said the baby and you are fighting for supremacy right now and he's winning."

Quinn looked over at Drew. He was sitting in one of his chairs facing her. He had his injured arm resting on a pillow. The room was dim and she could see out his windows that it was going on evening. She hadn't meant to lie down for quite so long.

"I seem to have taken up more time than I should have. I'm so sorry." She sat up slower this time and put her feet on the floor. She was surprised when he came over and sat next to her. She took the package of crackers when he held them out.

"I didn't have anything going on. Caroline cleared my calendar for the rest of the week anyway because of the accident." He pointed at the thermos on the floor. "Ice tea, no sugar, no lemon. If it's too warm I'm supposed to tell you Charlie will personally bring you some up to replace it. He said he's your slave."

"He's nuts is what he is. Thank you, I'm sure it's fine." Embarrassed for reasons she couldn't understand, she held the cold container in her hand. They sat there for several minutes not saying a word while she ate a cracker. Not because she was sick, but because she wasn't sure what she was supposed to do. She was about to get up and go when Drew spoke.

"I found your list." She looked at him, confused. "The one marked 'For the Prick.'"

She flushed. "You weren't supposed to see it. And I was mad when I wrote most of that." She started to stand up, but he grabbed her by the arm.

"You have every right to be mad at me. I'm an ass." She started to speak when he stopped her. "Please, let's talk, Quinn. I want...I would like us to discuss some of the things you have on your list."

She didn't know why he was being so nice and so...well, reasonable all of a sudden. But she wasn't going to fall for it. Her ex-husband used to—

"Why?" she demanded. "Why do you want to talk to me now when all you wanted to do before was yell and throw around orders like it was your job?"

He seemed to be thinking about something. She was sure it was about something she didn't want to know. When she walked over to the chair and started to gather her things up he came to stand beside her. Close. Too close, as far as she was concerned. Taking a step back, she nearly fell over the desk at her back. And would have if he hadn't reached out to steady her.

He didn't let her go. When she put her hands on his chest to push him back he groaned and she felt it rumble beneath her fingers. Then before she could think not to, she curled her fingers into his shirt rather than push him away.

"Quinn." Drew moaned before he lifted her chin with his fingers and gently brushed his mouth over hers. The second time his mouth touched hers she felt his hand slide up her neck. Even as she opened her mouth under his she could feel her body responding. Need coiled inside of her.

Tilting her head back and against his arm that was now wrapped around her, Quinn moved her hands down his chest and put her arms around his waist. He was hard; his cock rocked into her before he pulled back slightly. It was just enough to where she knew he was there, yet not where she could really feel him touching her.

He moved back from her slowly, his mouth gentled, then he lifted his head. Another kiss, powerful despite its briefness, left his taste in her mouth and along her lips. Tasting him now, running her tongue over her lips, she looked up at him when he moaned.

"How is it that you can do the simplest things and nearly bring me to my knees? I want you, Quinn. Right now and any way I can, but we need to talk." He stepped back, but didn't let go. "My arm is killing me and I'm hungry. I bet you are too."

"No. Yes. I…" She stepped away from him. "What's going on with you? You hate when I make lists, you usually yell at…who are you and what have you done with Drew?" She was startled by his bark of laughter. "I don't find any of this to be the least bit funny, Mr. Miller." She went around him and started gathering her things up again. When he just stood there and smiled she couldn't decide whether to be impressed with how handsome his smile made him or smack him. Holding out her hand, she glared at him. "My list, if you please. I'd like to get back home. I have things to do." When he continued to stare at her with that devastating smile, she huffed. "Damn it, what's wrong with you?"

"We are going to get something to eat, all right? Then we'll talk about your list. But for now…"

She was against him immediately, her body pressed against every bit of his. His fingers tangled in her hair as he deepened the kiss until she felt devoured, consumed, and conquered. This time when she wrapped her arms around him it wasn't so much as to touch, but to hang on, to keep from tumbling back to have him take her. Quinn had never been kissed like this, like she was wanted, needed even. When he pulled back this time she staggered and let him hold her. Not sure what had caused this change in him she was suddenly nervous. This man, this Andrew Miller, was confident in himself, more sure of her reactions to him. She looked up at him.

"Come on, love. Before we both end up on this floor." His voice was husky, dark, and deep. She didn't want to leave. "Quinn, you keep looking at me like that and I'm going to take you against that wall over there."

Quinn turned to look at the wall. When he chuckled she turned back and looked at him again. She could see lust in his eyes; need like her own was there as well.

"I don't understand you," she whispered. "Are you trying to make me crazy?"

He didn't answer her for a long time. She was beginning to think he wasn't going to when he finally did. "No. But you would be surprised if I told you what had happened. And before you stomp your foot and demand answers, I need to get a pain pill and you fed."

She immediately felt awful. It was the second time he'd mentioned the pain. She didn't want to hold him up from getting medicated when she could feed herself. She tried to pull away, but he simply held her.

"I'll go home. You go to your house and take something for the pain. I have my own car—"

"Quinn. You're going home with me and to eat. My parents have already made plans to meet you. We'll go…"

"I don't want to meet your parents," she squeaked. "You can just tell them…tell them you haven't seen me. I have to…you call them right now and tell them that—"

He kissed her. This one was different. It was more demanding, needier. His tongue didn't as much as swirl in her mouth, but invaded it. He pressed her hard against the wall she hadn't even realized they'd moved to and she moaned. Her body tightened and then expanded. Her breasts swelled and her nipples hardened and brushed erotically on the inside of her bra. When she reached her hand between them and cupped his hard cock in her palm he surged against her. He was so thick and long he filled her hand. When he tore his mouth from hers she felt his hot breath against her throat as his mouth nipped and bit at her.

"I want you, baby. Now. I want to be buried deep inside of you. Please, come home with me. I want to make love to you all night."

His mouth was doing sensual things to her. He was biting her throat and then her shoulder. She couldn't keep up with him. When she felt his hand slide under her skirt she nearly came right then.

"Drew, we shouldn't. We have to...yes." As his fingers brushed against her pussy she moved with him, rocking into him. When he slid inside of her she moved her legs wider as he moaned against her mouth.

"I need to taste you, Quinn. I need to lick you until you come in my mouth. Please, baby, I need you."

Suddenly, he was on his knees and before she could protest he had her skirt up over her hips and her panties moved to the side. The first brush of his tongue nearly had her screaming. As his fingers rocked inside of her she laced her fingers in his hair and held on. When he suckled her clit into his mouth and nipped she came apart.

Screaming out his name, she rode his mouth. Over and over she moved as his mouth continued to take her. When she came again, her body barely recovered from the first climax, her knees trembled with it. Suddenly he was standing before her, his cock rocking against her hard like he was fucking her.

"The desk, go to the desk and lean over it. I'm going to take you from behind, I can't...hurry," he said, his voice barely recognizable to her. "Christ, I need to be inside of you before I come like this."

On wobbly legs, she went to the desk, pulling her panties off as she went. She wanted to feel him there, his cock deep inside of her pussy. When she braced her hands on the desk Drew slid up behind her and she felt his cock at her entrance. Her breath caught when she felt the tip enter her.

"Please, Drew. Take me, please. I need you inside of me."

He pushed her head down to the desk then grabbed her hip. She'd be bruised tomorrow, but now all she could think of was him fucking her.

"Christ, you're so hot. I'm sorry, baby, but I can't wait. I'm so close to coming we'll be lucky if I don't enter you and come right now." As soon as his cock was seated in her she came. She pushed back against him every time he pulled back and then slammed deep. When she felt him stiffen, his cock deep inside, she knew he was coming and reached between her legs and cupped his balls.

His release was loud; he came yelling out her name. His hand at her hip held her tight and when he reached around, took her hand, and used her fingers with his to touch her clit, she came again. Shouting out his name and that she loved him.

For several seconds neither of them moved. As their bodies came back to earth and their hearts slowed Quinn realized what she'd said and wondered if he had heard. When he pulled her up from the desk and held her tight against him with his arm around her waist she leaned back against him. His cock, still semi-hard, was inside of her.

That's when she felt the sling. His arm. She'd probably hurt his arm. She started to pull away.

"No, please don't. Not yet. I just want to hold you for a minute. Please." He kissed her neck.

"What about your poor arm? I know what we did…that when you…Drew, you have to hurt." He laughed and she felt it rumble along her back.

"You only call me Drew when we have sex. I guess I can live with that." He ran his hand down her belly and spread his fingers wide over it. "How do you feel?"

She felt wonderful, relaxed and sated. But she was reasonably sure that wasn't what he meant. She pulled away this time and he let her. She was naked from her waist down and his pants were open and his cock wet with her juices. As she looked at him it shifted and stirred. She looked up at him when he laughed.

"My parents are probably wondering what we're doing. If you want me to take you again on the desk I will have to call them and let them know we've been…detained. Shall I?"

She flushed. "You most certainly will not. They probably have a very low opinion of me anyway."

His smile looked so sad for a second she was sure she'd imagined it. "You'd be surprised. But we really need to go. You have dinner with me and, if you still want to go home, I'll take you later, all right?"

She was so embarrassed that she nodded. Something had happened here tonight and she wasn't sure what. But she did know that it changed things. And not for the better.

CHAPTER 17

Robert got a ticket. He was still fuming about it when he got back to the pigsty and was in no mood to talk nice with his mother. She was sitting in the living room when he entered. It took him a few seconds to remember that he'd caused the mess in there and they hadn't been robbed.

"What have you to say for yourself, Robert? This mess has to be cleaned up and I'm not doing it. And you'll replace everything you've broken. Do you understand me?" She didn't move off the couch as she spoke. "I don't know what pissed you off this badly, but this will not happen again."

"Fuck off. You want it cleaned then you do it. I've got better things to do than be a house maid for you. Besides, none of this would have happened if you had paid the fucking cable bill and not got your hair done up. Which, by the way, looks like shit." He knew he'd scored a direct hit when she put her hand to her hair. "If you can't manage the money any better than that then perhaps I should take over the finances."

"Go ahead," she snapped. "I don't care. There isn't any more anyway. And at the end of next month there is less than nothing if Alyssa has her way." She got up, went over to the desk in the corner, and pulled open one of the drawers he'd missed. "Here are the bills that need to be paid and here is the income."

In one hand, there was a stack of bills at least three inches thick. In the other, there was nothing. Not even a checkbook. He looked up at her.

"The money for this month is gone. Between my hair, your dates, and your uncle's gambling, there isn't anything to pay bills with. So in less than ten days the power is going to be shut off, and sooner than that the phones will be off."

"That's not possible. It's only the..." He looked at his new watch he'd gotten the day before. "It's only the tenth. How the fuck can we be broke?"

"We only get ten grand a month each to live off of. And thirty thousand doesn't go as far as we're accustomed too. Of course we've never been on a budget before so I guess it's only natural that we haven't a clue how to live on one." Her laughter startled him. "And then we're going to be in real trouble starting the end of October."

He sort of remembered something about the twenty-eighth, but couldn't remember what. Robert thought it had something to do with Alyssa, but wasn't really sure what. At the time he'd been wondering how to get out of the fucking meeting, not paying attention to what was being said. Besides, he figured his mother and uncle were there, why did he have to pay attention?

"When Alyssa kicked us out of the house last year she had us sign that agreement stating that she would only give us an allowance for a year. That year, my dear son, is nearly over. She will cut us off as if we're nothing more than yesterday's old news."

"She can't do that. The will says that she is to provide us with our part of the estate. I remember that. It's like five million each. She can't just steal that from us too. She has to pay us our share." Robert sat down now, suddenly dizzy. "Doesn't she?"

His mother sat down too. "According to her attorney we spent all that and more when she was hiding out. My five million was spent within the first three years. Thankfully she was 'kind' enough to not count the credit card debt I'd incurred. You had gone through yours in less than a year. You've been, according to her attorney, living off her generously for over ten years. Your uncle wasn't given as much money so he blew through his in less time than you."

He couldn't breathe. Broke, they were broke? It wasn't possible. Nathan Howard was like this millionaire. And he'd left them well cared for. All of them.

"What about Nathan? Where's his money? He's been in that fucking sanitizer for over a year now. He has to have some money left." Robert would use that to make a fresh start. "Or is she keeping that money for herself too?"

His mother went through the bills in her hand and handed him one. It was from The Clinic. Robert knew it wasn't a sanitarium, but a place for drunks and drug addicts to dry out. He just called it that to piss his mother off. He opened the envelope.

Past due, it said. Forty thousand eight hundred dollars past due, as a matter of fact. Robert crumpled it up and tossed it on the floor.

"His money went to all those places he went to before Alyssa came back, she said, and she paid this one for one year. That's a bill for the next year of treatment, which I'm assuming she's not paying."

Robert got up and paced the cluttered room. Broke. They were all broke and soon to be homeless. He turned to his mother. "I suppose she's been paying the phone and other bills all along too." She nodded. "What else? What else has she been paying but won't now?"

"Your car will be repossessed next month along with any jewelry you've purchased since she's been footing the bill. Yes, that means your watch too."

He wrapped his hand around it. He glared at her. "You've known this all along. You've not paid the bills because you were trying to stick her with them. You fucking bitch."

She smiled and shrugged. "So what if I did? She'll have to pay them and I won't. Everything is in her name anyway."

His fist struck at her quick. Robert heard the crunch of bone, but didn't care. His temper was hot, red hot, and he didn't care to bring it down. As she fell off the chair he followed her to the floor. Over and over he pounded into her face and her ribs. He could see what he was doing; blood splattered over him and her too, but still he couldn't seem to stop, didn't want to stop. It wasn't until he was exhausted that he fell off her. His body spent, he lay back against the chair and closed his eyes.

This was Alyssa's fault too. She'd taken everything from them and made him lose his temper. He looked over at his mother and shuddered. She was in bad shape. Her face looked misshapen and broken. When he reached over and kicked her with the toe of his boot she didn't move, didn't make a sound.

"Mother, get up. You need to see a doctor. And you're bleeding on the floor. If you think I'm cleaning that up too, you can just forget it." He kicked her harder. "Get up." He was still sitting there when his uncle came home smelling of liquor and smoke. "She made me do it. She pissed me off about her daughter and I lost my temper."

Samuel leaned over and put his finger to her throat. Then he sat back on his heels and looked at him. Robert didn't like that look. It was the one he used when he was pissed about something someone had done and he'd have to figure out a way to get it cleaned up.

"What have you done, boy? What the hell have you done?" Samuel asked with a shake of his head. "She's dead. Your mother is dead."

Robert looked at her and then at his uncle. They both smiled. Not a friendly smile, Robert thought, but a smile that he'd scared people with.

"I think I just figured out a way to buy us more time in this house and maybe a bit more money. Grieving son and all," Robert said with a smirk. "Hot damn, but this might work out to our advantage, huh?"

His uncle smiled again. "You have got to be my son and not that other pansy-assed one she birthed and said was mine. Fuck, now we have to come up with a good story." Samuel looked around the room before he spoke again. "I'm thinking robbery, how about you?"

They worked on their story for nearly two hours. Then Robert cleaned up and they both left the house. Time to put plan "fuck the sister" into action.

~~~

Captain Cait Grant looked around the mess. There just wasn't any other way to describe it. The room had been destroyed and a woman murdered here. Her blood soaked the couch where she lay next to it and the carpet beneath her was sticky with the dark substance. Whoever had done this had been in a rage.

Cait looked over into the hallway at the two men standing there. They claimed they'd found the body. Something wasn't quite right about their story, but she couldn't put her finger on it just yet. She'd wanted to call her sister-in-law Dane to come and see what she could get from the scene and the men, but she and Jamie were on their second...or their third honeymoon.

The crime scene crew was waiting on the owner of the house. Alyssa Waite owned this house, as she did the ones on either side of it. Cait hated to do this to her, but the men were no help in knowing if anything had been stolen. Cait turned when she heard shouting in the hallway near the front door.

The Howard children, now adults, had been fighting since Cait had been just an officer on the force here in Columbus. Things hadn't changed much over the years as far as she could tell. The oldest boy, Nathan Howard the fourth, had been in and out of rehabilitation since he'd been a preteen. And as far as Cait knew that was where he was now. The younger boy, Robert Phillip Howard, was just trouble. She'd heard rumors that he had at least four bastard children and more aborted ones than she'd ever been able to get a count on. He had also been brought in on domestic violence a couple of times, but the girl usually decided not to press charges. Cait wondered if Mom had anything to do with that.

Alyssa, the baby of the family and the sole heir for the Howard estate, had done well for herself since she'd returned to the business. Cait had heard most of the story from the girl herself, but she was sure there was more than she'd been told. It wasn't until she'd met Cain Waite, Alyssa's new husband, that she'd been running the companies. Nickolas, Cait's brother-in-law, said that the girl was very smart about money and seemed to have a good head on her shoulders. That was saying a lot since Nickolas thought everyone was stupid with their money. Plus, Cain and Alyssa were good friends of theirs and had been over to their houses quite a bit lately.

Cait went to the doorway just as one of her officers was pulling out his weapon. Putting two fingers in her mouth and blowing, all movement stopped when she whistled.

"Now that I have your attention," Cait said with a grin. "Mrs. Waite, Doctor Waite, I'm really sorry about having to call you down here this late. Would you please wait for me in that room just over there?" Cait pointed to what looked like a dining room.

"Captain, this man here is armed," Carroll, one of her men, said with ill-disguised humor. "He said he was with the lady there." The large man in question winked at Cait. She knew he was the hired bodyguard for Alyssa. "He said that the only place she goes that he don't is the bedroom and the bathroom. Why do you suppose that is? He's kinda scary, isn't he?"

Cait had to fight a smile. Alyssa looked like she wanted to crawl in a hole and Cain looked like he was ready to explode with laughter. Cait nearly lost it when the guard, Ormond Carter, pulled out his knife and started to clean his nails.

"That's enough there, big guy," Cait said to Carter then she turned to Carroll. "Let the man go ahead with Mrs. Waite. She's been having some difficulties lately and he's to protect her."

Cait turned to Robert and Samuel Howard. Samuel looked too cool to have walked in on the gruesome scene she'd just witnessed and Robert much too polished. She'd bet her last dollar one or both of them had something to do with this.

"Gentlemen, why don't the two of you come with me? I'd like you to tell me what you—"

Robert cut her off. "Oh, for Christ's sake. Can't you get it from one of the other idiots we told this so?" Robert looked at his watch as he continued. "We've been standing here for nearly two hours waiting on Miss Money Bags to come here and now you want us to tell you what we saw again. I'm reasonably sure, Officer Grant, that we pretty much saw what you just did. My mother beaten to death and the room ransacked and things broken."

Cait didn't say anything as she processed what she'd just seen. Blood. There had been blood on the watch. Not a great deal, but enough that she could see it easily enough. Now she had to move with caution and care.

"Did you touch anything? Your mother or any of the things lying around the room?" She looked at both men as she asked. "Or maybe just the phone to call nine-one-one."

"Uncle Samuel felt her pulse. Said there wasn't any. Me? I just stayed the fuck out of the room once I saw the mess." Robert looked over at his uncle as he spoke. "Then I used my cell phone to call you, numbnuts."

Samuel took over from there. "We didn't touch anything else. I did check Shannon's pulse, as Robert said, but only to lay my two fingers on her throat. I couldn't find one and that's when I had him call."

They had rehearsed this. Tag team stories were a dead giveaway. They didn't overlap their telling and there was no pause from one narration to the next. Cait needed to separate these two quickly and get their statements. She'd bet any amount of money that their tale would be the same.

"Officer Carroll, could you take Samuel Howard down to the station and get his statement please?" Carroll moved forward. "Oh and get his finger prints for—"

"Finger prints? What the hell do you need our prints for? You can't think we had anything to do with this." Robert gave a panicky laugh. "Maybe we should call our lawyer. Uncle Samuel, what do you think?"

Cait waited for him to think things through. She had been dealing with bottom feeders like these two for a very long time. And she knew when someone just realized their partner in crime was too stupid to have around. She knew that Samuel would, if not today then very soon, throw his nephew under the bus to save his own hide.

"Maybe it would be best if we cooperate with the captain. I'm sure she had a good reason for wanting our prints." He looked at her. "Don't you, ma'am?"

"Of course. We'll need to separate yours from the assailant's. It will help us take all the innocents out of the equation." Cait smiled. "You wouldn't want us to arrest the wrong person, would you?"

She could see when he got it. When he knew she wasn't nearly as stupid or as naive as he'd first hoped she'd be. When Samuel turned and looked at Robert he simply nodded and then looked back at her. "I'm ready to go downtown now, officer. I'll be glad to give you any information you want."

Both Robert and Cait watched as Samuel was led out of the house. As they cleared the door two more people walked in—Andrew Miller and Quinn Waite. Cait nodded to the room where she'd sent Cain and Alyssa. Then she turned back to Robert.

"Who the fuck was that?" Robert snarled at her. "I'm not sure you should be letting all these people in my house. Maybe I should call someone. What's your badge number, by the way?"

"It isn't your house and my badge number is eight Charlie six." She pointed to the room at the other side of the door. "Why don't you have a seat in that room and I'll be right with you?" Nodding to the other officer, she had him stand with Robert. Robert was much too sure of himself now. Cocky almost. Cait went to the dining room to see the Waites.

CHAPTER 18

Drew hurt. And he knew that the pain was only going to get worse the longer he waited to rest his arm. He was beyond hiding the truth from Quinn. She seemed to have known that he was in too much pain to drive when they'd left the office earlier. She had simply taken the keys from him when they'd gotten to the parking lot and helped him into the passenger seat. They were just leaving the parking space when Cain had called to tell them what had happened.

"Shannon Howard was murdered at her home not long ago. Alyssa and I are on our way there now. Cait wants her to do a quick inventory to see if it might have been a case of interrupted robbery." He had lowered his voice. "She said it was bad."

Drew closed his eyes and reached for Quinn's hand as he put the phone on speaker and laid it on his leg. She took it immediately and held him. He knew that Alyssa hated her mother, but she was her mother nonetheless.

"How's Alyssa taking it? And we're on our way." Drew turned to Quinn. "Alyssa needs me to come to her mother's house, she was just murdered. Do you know the way?"

She nodded and turned left out of the lot. "Is there anything I can bring her, Cain? Do you have your bag?"

"Yes, I do. Nothing, she said, but thanks," Cain said to his sister. "Drew, if you hurt too much, I'm sure—"

"No. We're coming. Don't say anything until I get there. We should be there in…" Drew looked at Quinn.

"Ten minutes. Be safe." The call ended and Quinn glanced over at him. "I'm not sure if you know or not, but Alyssa's pregnant too. Three months."

He hadn't known. "No. I have to call my mom. I'm sorry about this, baby. I know we need to talk. I can't leave them to face this alone."

"Good heavens, Drew, I know that. I wouldn't want you to. Call your mother and I'll get us there." She brushed at a tear. "Poor Alyssa. He mother was a real piece of work, but to be murdered like—the police don't think she had anything to do with it, do they?"

Drew laughed at the venom in her voice. "No, they just want her to rule out robbery. It's Alyssa's house and for the most part, so is everything in it. You're very protective of her, aren't you?"

"She saved my life. And I love her."

Drew thought about what Quinn had said…shouted really, when she'd climaxed. She loved him. She'd said she loved him. He picked up his phone and dialed his grandda's house. Drew's dad answered on the first ring. He told his dad what had happened.

"That poor girl. Give her my…hang on, your mother is asking me something." Drew could hear the mumble of someone's voice, but not who it was or what was being said. "Give us the address. Your mother has it in her head that your girl hasn't eaten since she got sick. She wants to bring her something."

Drew was about to tell him no, he'd take care of her when he saw Quinn put her hand over her belly. "All right. But bring me something too. And one of those pain pills. I'll take half of one and that should work."

Five minutes later, they were in the driveway with perhaps ten other vehicles, mostly police and ambulances. There was also a coroner van. Quinn got out of the car and stood nearby while his father continued talking.

"You both need to get some rest. After this is over, your mom and I want you to come stay with us a few days. Work things out before you sit down with Quinn."

"We've been talking…well, sort of. She has a list. She called it the 'For the Prick' list." His dad laughed. "I asked her to come to the house with me. That's where we were headed when this came up."

His dad laughed again. "Sex is good. It usually solves a lot of problems with your mom and me. I used to get her mad just to—"

"Dad! Too much. Please." He laughed when his dad did.

"So, son, have you figured it out yet?"

Drew glanced at Quinn. He wanted to pretend he didn't know what he was talking about, but that would just be stupid when they both knew he would be lying. "You mean that I love her?" His dad laughed harder. "Yes. She loves me too, by the way."

"Sure she does. You're a Miller, aren't you?" His dad lowered his voice as he continued. "The whole reverse psychology thing was your grandda's idea. Said you'd bite hook, line, and sinker. Guess he was right, huh?"

Drew looked at Quinn as he answered his dad. "Yeah, I guess he was. But let's not tell him that." His dad agreed.

Now he was sitting here waiting with Alyssa and Cain. Cain was quiet, but Alyssa and Quinn were talking quietly at the other end of the table.

Drew looked at Cain. They hadn't really spoken since they'd had that fight in the hospital last week. He hoped they'd be able to work out the differences soon. He really missed him. When Cait stepped into the room, they both stood up.

"Drew, your parents are here. I know your dad is an attorney too. Is he here on business or something else?"

"They're bringing Quinn some food. She...we were going to my house for dinner when Cain called." Cait nodded. "And to also bring me something for pain."

Cait let them in and as they started emptying what looked like everything in the refrigerator at his grandda's house, Cait told them what she knew and some of what she suspected.

"At first glance it looks like a simply break-in gone sour. But there are a couple of things that...well, I think it's something more now. And I don't know where to go with it."

"Cait, is my mother, is she really dead?" Alyssa asked. Drew watched as Cain picked her up and sat her on his lap.

"Yes, honey, I'm afraid so. The coroner is getting her ready to transport to the hospital now. They have to do an autopsy, of course, but she's gone. I'm so sorry."

Drew spoke up as his mom set a huge plate of food in front of Quinn. "You don't have any suspects then, do you?"

There was a tug of war going on between Quinn and his mom, but Quinn held her own for as long as she could. Drew thought his dad was going to hurt himself trying not to laugh.

"Well…I do and I don't. Your brother, Alyssa, what do you know about him? Anything come to mind? Especially recently?" Cait asked as she took a cupcake off the platter.

Alyssa shook her head. "No. I've actually only seen him a couple of times in the last year. My mother also for that matter. Only when they thought they wanted something I wasn't giving them. She's been to the office a few times. But I had her…she's been escorted out by security each time she came by."

Drew took the half pain pill his mom handed him and the glass of tea. He noticed that Quinn was picking at the food his mom had given her, but she would cast a dirty look at them every chance she got. Drew's dad just watched both the women with an odd smile.

"I'm going to have to canvas the neighbors to see if anyone saw anything. Then I'm going to question you—"

"You know," Quinn shouted across the room, "I know something that might be helpful if anyone cares to come down here and take some of this food I don't want to eat but am being forced to."

Drew looked at his dad when he started laughing. When he quickly turned it into a coughing fit Drew didn't have to turn around to know that his mom was glaring at him. Quinn started drumming her fingers on the table and glared too. She looked beautiful, he thought, even when she was pissed off.

Cait didn't bother hiding her laughter. If anything, she seemed to laugh harder every time someone looked at her. Including his mom.

"Oh all right. But you will eat more in the morning at breakfast, young lady," Rose huffed as she sat down again. "You're much too skinny as it is now and I won't have my grandchild suffer because you think you're too fat."

Quinn was up in a heartbeat. "Listen here, Mrs. Miller, I will eat when I want, what I want, and however much I want. You are not my...you are not... Oh Christ, I'm gonna be sick again." She fled the room with her hand over her mouth.

Drew and Cain both leapt to their feet to go after her, but Rose held up her hand to stay them. "Let me go. It seems, Drew, your little girlfriend has a great deal more backbone than I thought. I think I'll grow to love her as much as you do."

With that she swept out of the door after Quinn. Drew looked at his dad when he started clapping. Drew put his

174

head on the table. He didn't think he'd ever understand women. He wasn't even sure he wanted to.

~~~

Rose went out the door behind Quinn. The girl was gone, she saw, and that was when she noticed the two officers in the hall looking out the front door and laughing. She went toward them.

"Did Miss Waite go by here?" One of them nodded, a smirk on his face. "You know, having morning sickness isn't funny, young man. That girl is carrying my grandchild and you'd do well to remember who I am."

"And who would that be, ma'am? Somebody important by any chance? The queen or something?" He laughed and turned to his partner who was no longer laughing, but wisely backing away. "I know, you're the president of the U.S. of A."

"No, but you're close. I'm the woman who does things to fuck-head cops like you to make them wish for their mommies. I'm in charge of Internal Affairs of the State of Ohio, you dunderhead." She watched his face as it hardened and fury replaced his humor.

"I haven't done anything wrong but laugh at a stupid girl who got herself knocked up. You can't fault a guy for having a bit of fun."

"No," Cait said from behind her, "but I can. Vernon, you've been a pain in my ass since I took you in."

Rose went to find her future daughter-in-law, confident that Officer Vernon was in good hands. Rose heard Quinn before she found her. Quinn was standing near the side of the house crying.

"Here." Rose handed her a few tissues and a package of crackers. "I lived on those when I was pregnant with Andrew. I think Tommy, his father, bought stock in the company and made us very rich for the first nine months we owned the stock."

Quinn blew her nose before speaking. "Anyone ever tell you you're a pain in the ass, Mrs. Miller?"

Rose grinned. "Once or twice. Do you think you could drop the Mrs. Miller crap and call me by my given name? I know it's supposed to be respectable, but I think you're just trying to get a rise out of me." Rose sat on the ground next to her. "Eat the cracker, Quinn."

They sat there for several minutes while Quinn nibbled on the crackers. Rose looked out over the yard and noticed that the neighbors were beginning to be questioned by the other officers. Rose remembered what Quinn had said before she'd run out of the house. But before she could ask, Quinn spoke up.

"I'm not going to marry Drew. I know that I should for the child, but I won't." She ate another bite of cracker. "I was married once before. He was...he wasn't such a great choice."

Rose didn't know what to say for a few seconds. To buy time she leaned back on her hands and regarded the girl, stunned at the revelation. "So you don't love Andrew. That's really too bad because he loves you." Rose nearly smiled at the look of shock on her face. Quinn didn't know, which wasn't really surprising. The two of them didn't seem to say much to one another.

"No, you're wrong. He can barely stand me most...he hates me. He hates my ideas, my...I make lists and he gets so angry about them. He gets pissed about everything I do. No, Mrs. Mil…Rose, you're wrong."

"Do you love him, Quinn?" Rose asked her quietly.

Quinn ate another cracker before she answered. Rose would never forget the answer for as long as she lived. And she was sure that she'd laugh every time.

"He makes it damned hard to even like him most of the time, the stubborn duckweed. But I never would have sex with him if I…I think I've loved him all my life." Quinn stood up and brushed crumbs off her skirt. "And you're pretty slick. But not so good that I didn't notice you pumping me for information that is frankly none of your business. But it doesn't matter. I'm not marrying your son."

Rose sat on the grass and grinned as Quinn stalked away toward the street. Rose thought she was going to enjoy this girl once she figured out that Drew actually loved her and they were finally married. She got up to go inside. Yes, she thought, it was never going to be a dull moment with her around.

She was about to the doorway again when a man exploded out and right into her. Rose wasn't sure what had happened as she was thrown ass over head onto the ground. She was ready to blast the clumsy idiot when she felt the bite of the gun at her temple.

"Fucking don't move, bitch. Come with me and I won't hurt you," the voice behind her snapped.

"If you don't want me to move how do you expect me to come with you?" She knew she shouldn't have said it, but he'd pissed her off by knocking her down.

The cuff to the side of her head had her seeing stars. It took her a few seconds longer to focus on the shouting going on around her. Then she felt the gun at her head again as the man held her in front of him.

"Let Mrs. Miller go and we'll talk this over. No one needs to get hurt." Cait? Rose tried to focus on seeing who was speaking, but there was something in her eyes. She knew in that second that she was bleeding.

"Yeah right, bitch. You're not gonna pin my mother's murder on me. Uncle Samuel just texted me and said you got a witness. Tell me who the cock sucker—stay back. I'll shoot her." Rose was tired of being tossed around like a rag doll and glared at the man in the uniform who was now backing away.

"Let me go, you idiot. They'll simply shoot me to get to you. And I'm in too good a mood to let you be the cause of me getting shot." Rose started to twist around and toss his ass to the ground when another voice, this one much softer and a great deal more confident, spoke.

"Let her go and I won't blow your fucking head off."

CHAPTER 19

Quinn decided that if all she did was throw up for the next eight months then this was going to be a one shot deal. Her belly cramped again, but so far that's all she'd done since they'd brought her to the hospital. She brushed her teeth again.

She left the tiny bathroom and made her way back to the bed. The nurse kept tisking at her about keeping the gown closed, but she had a headache and her mouth hurt. She didn't give a crap if her ass hung out a little.

Just as she was covering back up the curtain flew back and she was engulfed into someone's arms. Cain. She could tell by the way he smelled. Before she could hold him too, he let her go. Then Alyssa held her. Tears went unchecked down her cheeks as they, Cain and Alyssa, starting talking at once.

"Are you all right?"

"Did he hurt you?"

"What the fuck were you thinking?" That was from Cain.

Before she could answer the other side of the curtain was thrown back and was ripped from the rod. Quinn wasn't sure she'd ever seen Drew look this mad before.

"That's something I'd like an answer to, actually. What the fuck were you thinking, or were you?" Drew snarled at her. "Do you have any idea what he might have done to you?"

"Yeah, I did. But he didn't, did he? So back the fuck off, buck-o." She had a second to realize that they had an audience, but quickly dismissed them. "Oh and by the way, you're fucking welcome, you overgrown ass."

"Welcome. Welco...are you insane? What do you think in that tiny, pea-sized brain of yours I could possibly have to thank you for?" He took two steps toward her as she climbed back out of the bed. "Except for giving us all a fucking heart attack."

"I saved your mother, you nincompoop. In case you forgot that little tidbit. That guy had a gun to her head." She was shouting now too. "He was going to kill her."

"Oh and you thought you were so much better equipped to handle the situation than the...I don't know, fifty cops with guns could do?" He was close enough now that she could feel the heat of his anger. "When we get married, you're going to—"

Anger made her voice low and hard. "I wouldn't marry you if you were the last man on earth."

That shut him up. His mouth snapped closed so quickly she heard his teeth click together. But it didn't seem to cool his temper any.

"Yes, you are. As soon as it can be arranged, as a matter of fact. Today, if I can manage it."

"Drew," Alyssa started. "I don't think—"

"Good. Stay out of this. This is between the two of us. She needs a keeper and I'm going to make sure she stays safe even if I have to tie her to the bed to make sure she is." When Cain stepped forward Drew stopped him. "I mean it, Cain. I won't let her hurt my child."

Quinn felt the air leave her lungs. Her heart crushed under the weight of the pain. The baby. He was only worried she'd hurt his baby. She couldn't speak so she turned to the bed and slowly climbed back in. She knew that Drew and Cain were still talking, but she no longer cared. It wasn't until Alyssa came over and took her hand that she looked around. They were alone in the curtained off area.

"He didn't mean it, Quinn. He was just scared. Men can say the stupidest things when they're frightened." Quinn didn't speak. "Quinn, honey, he loves you."

Alyssa kept talking to her, but she wasn't listening. Not really anyway. She heard Alyssa say that Cait was coming in to take her statement. That she'd stay with her if she wanted. And that she didn't blame her for being upset.

When Cait arrived an hour later Quinn had her mental list complete. She knew what she needed to do and how she was going to do it. But first things first.

"Alyssa, do you think you could get one of the nurses to bring me something to eat? I'm starved." Alyssa smiled at her and Quinn hoped her smile didn't look as forced as it felt. "All I've done is throw up for a week and suddenly I want some food."

"Sure. I'll even have Cain go and get you your favorite. I'll be right back." Suddenly, she was gone.

"Smooth move there, Waite. You do know she's probably going to bring you back half the store, right? And I would have gotten rid of her for you if you wanted." Quinn ignored her for the moment. She'd always thought that Captain Grant was way too observant for a regular cop anyway.

"I have no idea what you mean." She settled back against the bed. "I was told you had questions fo—"

Mrs. Miller barged right in and swooped down on her. Quinn wasn't sure when she'd become a hugger, but as far as hugs went this one felt good; more than good, it felt wonderful.

"Oh, darling, you're all right. When I heard you speak so calmly behind me I just knew you were going to be so brave. There's no telling what he might have…I'm so glad you're all right." As she hugged her again Quinn looked at Captain Grant, who smiled.

"Mrs. Miller, I need to take Miss Waite's statement. I'm sure you understand, under the circumstances, that I need to have the least amount of people around as possible. Maybe on your way out you can ask the others to give us a bit of time."

"Oh yes, of course. I've already given mine to that other officer, Officer Carroll, I believe." Rose hugged her again. "Thank you, my dear. I can't…thank you."

After she left, Cait didn't say anything for a couple of minutes. Quinn didn't care. She was hurting and it wasn't just from her injurers either. Quinn decided to get it over with.

"I was walking back to the house to tell Drew…it doesn't matter about what I was going to say to him anymore." Quinn rolled to her side as she continued. "I could see that you guys were all on the porch, but I couldn't see what was going on. I thought you'd been sent to find me."

"When did you realize that there was a hostage situation?" Quinn turned when she heard something click. "I hope you don't mind that I'm going to record this. I want to make sure I get your statement right the first time."

Quinn shook her head and rolled back to her side. She closed her eyes and could see what had happened as if it were a movie and she was watching it rather than living it.

"His back was to me. I couldn't tell who he was, but when he jerked around I heard Mrs. Miller tell him to let her go. She told him that they'd shoot her before they let him go." Quinn turned to Cait. "Would they have shot her?"

Cait laughed. "No. Tempting, but no. She was bluffing. Then what?"

"I walked up behind him and told him to let her go and I wouldn't hurt him." She thought about what she'd actually said and amended it. "I told him I wouldn't blow his fucking brains out."

He'd stiffened, she saw. His back actually stiffened before he spoke. "You think you can shoot me before this woman is dead, then go right ahead and try."

Quinn only had a small stick, one she'd picked up as she walked up behind the man. She jabbed it into the back of his head hoping he'd not figure out what it was and that she was bluffing.

"Okay. Any last words before I pull the trigger? Oh and is your will up to date?" Quinn poked him again. "From this angle I can't miss that tiny little brain you're currently not using."

"I didn't do anything. That bitch on the porch took my uncle downtown and now he's saying they got a witness that says I killed my mother." He took a step back, but didn't relinquish his hold on Rose. "I just had to get away and think. Then this woman got in my way and slowed me down."

Quinn snorted. "And you believed him? Let me guess, he's saying they know you did it and he's trying his best to tell them you didn't. So how do you know that his witness isn't himself and that he knows all the details 'cause he killed her? And now he's trying to pin it on you."

The man, she knew now, was Alyssa's brother, Robert Howard. Quinn had never met the man, but she knew plenty about him. He was a shiftless bastard who hurt women for pleasure. And he'd hurt her friend and sister-in-law too.

"Let Mrs. Miller go and...and you can take me with you." She heard someone shout at her to back off, but she took a step toward Robert. "Nobody up there cares if you kidnap some older woman, but they will when you take an heiress. My family invented...we invented Velcro. Ever heard of it?" Quinn didn't have a clue what she was saying, but she was stalling until she could convince him to let Rose go. She didn't know who invented Velcro and she was hoping he didn't either.

"Of course I have. You'd have to be a real idiot to not know what that was. And you're stupid if you think I don't know who invented it too. It was a Swiss electrical engineer named George de Mestral. I did go to college. You don't look Swiss or the daughter of an engineer."

He turned around and the gun came out from behind Rose's head so quickly that Quinn had no time to hide her "weapon." Now the gun, his gun, was pointed at her. But he still had Rose trapped between them.

"A stick? A fucking stick? You thought you'd get me to let her go and come with you with a stick to my head?" He lunged at her the same time Quinn yanked Rose's arm down and threw her behind her.

"Yeah it would have worked too if you'd just left her the fuck alone." Quinn didn't hesitate, but brought her head forward and tried to hit him in the forehead with hers. But he shifted, whether from the loss of Rose or what, but she missed and hit him in the shoulder instead.

As he brought he gun back up toward her Quinn grabbed his extending arm and pushed it down hard as the gun went off. Bringing his arm back up she twisted it around, shifting him to her back, and yanked his arm over her shoulder as she bent at the knees and flipped him over her shoulder. He landed on his back with a thud. Scrambling to get his gun he grabbed her leg and she dropped to the ground, hitting her head and mouth on something hard. Before she could bring the gun up that she had managed to reach Robert came apart before her eyes.

Quinn opened her eyes and then looked over at Cait. "He was being shot, wasn't he?"

"Yes," Cait answered softly. "All of us opened fire on him as soon as we had a clear shot. Up until then either you or Mrs. Miller was in the way."

Quinn nodded as she rolled back over. "I guess it was really stupid of me to risk Mr. Miller's baby, wasn't it? You guys had it under control all along." Cait didn't answer.

Drew...Mr. Miller had been right, she'd been incredibly stupid. And she suddenly felt useless. She remembered the reason she'd been upset with them in the house. "There's a security system in the house. It's in each of the rooms and records twenty-four-seven. I know that they didn't know about it because I'm sure they would have disabled it had they known. It's in a safe behind the furnace. I...I didn't put it in, but the previous owners called about three weeks after the Howards had moved in to tell me." Quinn waited for Cait to say something. When she didn't, she went on. "I would go in with the cleaning lady once a week to change out the DVDs. It was set up on a seven disc changer that would move to the next one every day. They're still there, all of them. I've marked and dated them every time."

Quinn shifted on the bed, thinking about how much Drew would be angry about her going into the house and then marking and dating the DVDs. Cait brought her out of her musings.

"When was the last time you changed them, Quinn?"

She had to think. She wasn't even sure what the date was right now. "I was...the cleaning lady came in on

Wednesdays. So then, I guess. I only have six left. I should have purchased more when I was out this week. Maybe I will tomorrow." Quinn was suddenly very tired. The pain where her heart had been wouldn't ease up and she wondered if it ever would. Something else occurred to her. "You'll need the combination. It's zero, three, zero, four, twelve, right, left, right." Cait repeated it back. "Yes, that's correct. Cait, I'm very tired. Do you think it would be too much trouble to have them leave me alone for a bit? I would like to take a nap." Quinn was asleep before Cait answered.

CHAPTER 20

Drew went in to check on Quinn before he left to go home. He hurt still and he needed to change. He was covered in blood from dragging Quinn into his arms when he'd found her with Cain. She'd already fainted by then and he'd never been so frightened in his life. The medic said her head was fine, but he'd had her taken to the hospital anyway. He was worried about the baby and her too much not to.

Kissing her gently on the forehead, he left. There was a guard outside of her room now. He smiled. Quinn hadn't even stirred when she'd been transported to the private room she was in now. Cain had told him she was fine but exhausted. Drew was dizzy himself. As he made his way up to his bedroom at his grandda's, he realized they'd been up for over forty-eight hours. His father gave him a pain pill and a promise to wake him at noon. Glancing at his watch, Drew couldn't believe it was five in the morning.

His last thought before sleep claimed him was that it had been a hell of a night.

It was ten after twelve when his father woke him. He had the strangest look on his face, but Drew didn't question it. He knew it had been a strange night for them all. He got up and went in to take a shower. When he came out with his robe on his dad was still sitting on the chair.

"Dad?"

"She's gone. Left without telling us last night, I guess. They have a few people looking for her. I have a few looking myself, but she's gone." He put his head in his hands and continued. "Your mother is upset. The hospital didn't even call us to let us know. They told us that as she's no relation to us they weren't required to tell us anything."

Drew sat down on his bed. Gone? He knew he was going to regret asking, but he needed to be sure.

"Who's gone, Dad? Tell me who left without a word."

His dad looked up. "Quinn. Quinn left AMA. She was going to be released sometime today. But I guess that doesn't matter anymore."

Against Medical Advice. Drew stood up. Why would she leave? Didn't she realize that he'd be picking her up today, bringing her to his house? He needed to keep her safe, protected.

He picked up his cell phone next to the bed and saw he had missed calls. He was surprised to find that he had eighteen of them and most of them were from Alyssa. He punched in her number and when she answered, he knew something else had gone wrong.

"She left. Damned girl left. And they won't tell me where she's at. Can you believe they have the…where are you at?"

"Home. Who won't tell you? What's going on?" His mother walked in as he was asking. "Tell me what you know. Don't leave anything out, all right? Where, Alyssa?"

Alyssa sighed and even through the phone he could tell she was pissed. "Those damned Grant women. They won't tell me a damned thing. And Cait! How could an officer of the law…damn it, damn it. We're worried, don't they care? All they'll tell me is…Cain is fit to be tied. He's called their husbands."

Drew was trying to sort through what she was saying when his grandda walked in with Cait. Drew had a moment to wonder if everyone in the household was going to come into his bedroom when he looked at the envelope in Cait's hand.

"Let me call you back." He closed the phone on Alyssa and stared at the two newcomers. "What is it, Cait? Why won't anyone tell me where she is?"

Cait grinned. It wasn't a particularly friendly grin, but one that said, "I know something you don't and I'm glad for it."

"You want this, then call off Cain. Now. It's from Quinn."

Drew didn't even question her, but dialed Cain. "Stop bothering the Grants. I mean like yesterday."

"They fucking know where she is and won't tell me. And if you don't give a shit where she is, I most certainly do. She was my sister long before she was your fuck partner."

Drew knew that he deserved that. Hell, if he had a sister and Cain had done that to her he'd be hard pressed not to castrate him. But Cait had something he needed and he would do anything to get it.

"Cait is here now with an envelope from Quinn. She won't give it to me until you back the fuck off. So I'm asking…I'm begging you to back the fuck off."

Drew waited. He knew that the man was struggling. Cain was pissed at him and probably blamed him for her being gone. He'd only wanted to protect her and keep her safe and she'd run off.

"All right. But I'm coming over and I'm reading the letter. If you want my help then you'll agree. I'm not particularly happy with you at the moment and it won't take much persuasion for me to knock you on your fucking ass."

"Deal. But if it's about us and our sex life then you asked for it. And I have a few things to say to Quinn myself." Drew didn't know why he was provoking the man, but he was pissed too.

Cain laughed. "Oh I heard about how you told her what she was going to be doing. I've no doubt this is all about you and you wanting to save her baby and not her." The phone went dead before he could make a comment.

He looked around the room and the people assembled there. "He's doing it now. And he's coming over. Can I have the letter, Cait?"

"No. Not until I hear from my sisters-in-law. I'll be downstairs. You might want to get dressed. You're about to have company." She left the room, and his grandda with her.

Drew looked over at his dad and mom. "Cain said that I told her I was only out to protect my child and not her. That's not what I said."

"Actually, it is," his mother said, a bit of anger in her voice. "Alyssa said you told her that you needed to protect the baby even if she didn't. I believe your exact words were, 'I won't let you hurt my child.' Sort of implying that you didn't think she was capable of protecting it on her own." His mother left too.

Had he? He wasn't sure if that was what he'd said, but it wasn't what he'd meant. He looked over at his dad. He was looking at him like he had the time he'd been caught drunk at a party where there was supposed to be adults and there weren't. Drew and his friends had only been fifteen at the time. Drew hated that look.

"Dad, I didn't—"

"Maybe not, but you did." His dad stood and so did he. "Son, I've been proud of you all my life, even when you pissed me off so badly I wanted to beat you until you couldn't sit for a week. But right now...right now all I can think about is that my grandchild is out there with his mother and I think he might be better off without you."

He walked out of the room and shut the door behind him. Drew could only stare at it. Christ, what had he done that had been so bad? He'd agreed to marry her, hadn't he? He stood up to finish getting dressed.

He'd even agreed to provide her with...well, they hadn't gotten to what he was going to provide her with, but he—

Drew stopped dead in his tracks. Had he done that? Had she agreed to anything? He tried to think. He'd asked her to marry him, right? No, he hadn't, he realized after a few minutes of thinking. He'd told her that…well, it was for the best. His child was going to need… His child. Not their child, but his. He started to pull on his pants one handed when he realized that he'd never once referred to the baby as theirs. Was that really any reason to get pissed off? He wasn't sure now.

Other things he'd said, implied, came to him. He'd told her that she needed protecting. She'd saved his mom. Not that there weren't others around more capable, more armed, but she'd jumped right in and done it despite the odds against her. He had told her she wasn't doing a good job at being pregnant either. Not in those words, but he'd said it. Drew was halfway down the stairs when he had to sit down. He'd never even told her that he loved her, not even after he'd figured it out several days ago. He looked up as Cait sat down next to him.

"Hard to admit when you fuck up, huh?" She handed him the envelope. "I don't know where she is. My sisters, they arranged the entire thing so that you'd have this epiphany. I was sure you weren't going to, but I've been wrong before."

Drew snorted, a habit he'd picked up recently. "I'm sure you don't tell that to Spencer much."

Cait laughed. "Nope, and if you tell him I said it I'll have every cop in the state looking for you to ticket you. I'm sorry, Drew. Good luck."

She stood and moved down the rest of the stairs and toward the door. Cain was just raising his hand up when she opened it. She said a few words to him, low so that Drew couldn't hear, then pointed up at him. Alyssa came in behind them. She went to the living room where Drew assumed everyone else was and Cain went to the stairs.

"Cait said you had a breakthrough. That true?" Cain sat down next to him. "I'd like to think my sister has better sense than to hook up with someone so stupid, but there's no accounting for taste I suppose."

Drew handed the sealed envelope to Cain. "I suppose. I've thought that about Alyssa too." Neither man spoke for several minutes.

"Are you in love with Quinn, Drew? I mean really in love with her and not the fact that she's carrying your child?"

Drew knew that this was the turning point in their relationship. "Yes. And I think that I've loved her a great deal longer than I ever knew. And just for the record, it's not my child, it's ours. Hers and mine."

Cain laughed, a bark of laughter that soon turned into a full belly laugh. His family came from the living room as Drew joined him.

"I guess I need to welcome you to the family then." Cain stood and put out his hand. "Let's go find her. Together."

Drew took his hand and stood. He was pulled into a huge bear hug that made him wince. The man could hug like nobody Drew knew.

CHAPTER 21

"Mr. Miller,

As you have noticed, I'm no longer at the hospital. I won't go into details as to how I left, but I will tell you why.

I left because frankly, I don't like you very much. And as you and I don't seem to get along very well I'm sure you'll understand that we would never work as a married couple. But we do have a child together.

I won't keep you from the baby. I'm not the monster you seem to think I am and I wouldn't do that to either you or the child. I will also keep you informed via a lawyer about the progress of my pregnancy and anything about said child.

Stay away from me. Please.
Quinn S. Waite"

Tommy read the letter again and tried very hard not to admire the girl. She had spunk, he'd give her that. He grinned when he thought about her taking on an armed man when his wife had been in his clutches. Yep, Tommy thought, he was going to enjoy having her as a daughter. He looked up when his wife sat next to him.

"She's got him in a twist, doesn't she?" Tommy nodded at Rose. "I'm going to enjoy watching these two together. How about you?"

Tommy smiled bigger. "I was just thinking the same thing. Do you think we should tell him where she is?"

Tommy had had several private detectives watching her for several days now. He'd known the moment she'd left the hospital and with whom. The Grant women were a scary bunch and he hoped to never cross one of them.

The women, all five of them, minus the cop, had gone to the hospital about an hour after Drew had left according to the report he'd been given. When they left they'd been a party of seven. Mrs. Parker had shown up not long after they got there and had a car waiting out front for them. His men had lost them twice and only figured out they'd taken Quinn to the airport because his pilot had noticed the Grant jet sitting on the tarmac when Tommy had called and asked him if he could walk around the hub and keep an eye out for the women.

"Strange thing, Mr. Miller," the pilot, Augustus, had said. "But the Grant plane is all gassed up and sitting here running. Don't know the pilot of that thing, but it sure is a biggin."

"Do you think you can find out for me where it might be headed? It's very important to Drew." Tommy hadn't wanted to get his hopes up, but it was just too opportune that they would be spiriting off a woman and the plane was ready to go.

"Ah, sure. Let me take a walk over and strike up a convo for a bit. Maybe the guy's a talker. Can't hurt to find out now, does it?" He called Tommy back twenty minutes later. "They's headed to Tennessee. Nashville. Ever been, Mr. Miller? Would like to go myself sometime and take the missus. She always had a thing for the singer that died a while back."

Tommy was so grateful that he promised Augustus that he and his wife would go on vacation there as soon as it could be arranged. And he'd foot the bill. It took him another hour to figure out Quinn had a sister down there. By the time he had her address in Nashville, Quinn was already landing. Tommy went to his son's room to wake him at noon not ten minutes after he'd gotten off the phone with another group of men to watch her there.

"No. It won't hurt him to stew in his own juices for a bit longer. Besides, I think the girl needs to do some thinking on her own. It's been a whirlwind of a last few days." Rose looked at her husband. "I can't help but be proud of her. She certainly isn't going to take any shit from him, will she?"

Tommy laughed and as the room glanced his way, he sobered up. "No. And I'm betting he'll be a better man because of her."

It was nearly five that evening before the others figured it out. Tommy acted as surprised as the rest of them had when they did. Secretly he had hoped it would be at least another day, but was glad for them. He'd been about to bust with the knowledge.

But he did plan to pull his son aside and have him talk with another woman. He didn't know her very well, but

from what he'd been able to find out, he thought that
Drew should speak to Morgan Grant.

~~~

Drew hoped his dad was satisfied. He'd been sitting in
this room for over twenty minutes waiting on Mrs. Grant
to talk to him. She'd had an emergency and had had to
deal with it first. He didn't know what it could be, but
waited. The front doorbell had rung several times since
he'd been sitting here.

He'd met Morgan a few years ago at a fundraiser. His
grandda had wanted to go and didn't want to have to find
a woman to go with. Drew had actually met all the Grant
women then, including the matriarch, Mrs. Margaret
Parker. There was a scary woman, he thought with a
smile.

When the door opened to the study, Drew stood up.
He nearly bolted to the door when the same women he'd
been thinking about all walked in. All of them.

"If this is a bad time I can…why don't I come back
when you'rr less…when you can see me alone. I just came
here because I…my dad…fuck." Drew flushed when the
elder woman huffed at him.

"Your parents, I'm sure, taught you better manners
than that," Mrs. Parker said with a look as she sat down
and nodded to the other women.

"Yes, ma'am, she did." Drew remained standing until
the women all sat down. He eyed the door and when Cait
laughed, he turned to her.

"You'll never make it. Sit down, Drew. Morgan said
that you were going to go after your pregnant girlfriend
and that you needed advice." She went to the bar and

brought him back a tumbler full of amber liquid as he continued standing. "You might need this."

"I'm sure you ladies will understand that I think I should just go and get her. She and I need to talk, that's all. I'm sure that we can get a lot accomplished that way." He looked at the door again.

"And what will you say to her once you see her? I'm curious only because you seem like a reasonably intelligent man. What will you say about the baby she's carrying and her plans to let you into her life?" Drew thought her name was Dane. "Yes, I'm Dane."

He sat down hard. He'd heard stories about this Grant woman. She'd been helpful in all sorts of cases of missing children over the years. He'd also heard that she was a billionaire as well.

"The stories are for the most part true. But it's not only children I find, but adults as well. It doesn't always end well, but James, my husband, is there for me every night, as are our three children." She sat closer to the end of the couch and reached her hand out to him. "Would you like to know when you're going to die, Drew?"

He'd been reaching out to take her hand and snatched it back so quickly he hurt his wound. He glared at her when she laughed at him.

"Behave, Dane. She can't tell you when you'll die. She's being mean to you. I'm Taylor by the way. Byron is my husband." She smiled at him. "You didn't answer the question. What are you going to say to her when you get to her? Because I'll tell you right now, if we're not all satisfied with your answer we'll simply hide her again."

He knew in that moment that they had helped Quinn. He sat down on the couch and looked at them all. He was in the presence of great beauty and wealth. He looked around the room and wondered what their husbands did to keep them so happy-looking. Drew was in over his head, not just with these women, but the one he only just discovered he loved.

"I'm going to beg her to forgive me. I'm going to tell her every day, every minute, and every second of every day that I don't deserve her and that I love her." He leaned back on the couch and took a deep breath. "I don't suppose you ladies would mind giving a fool some help in keeping his wife…future wife, as happy as you all are, would you?"

"That's a good start, young man. A very good start. My Dan, bless his soul, used to bring me flowers and candy for no reason at all. Made my week when he did that. My sons do it for me now and again, but it's not the same as when it's from your spouse." Margaret looked around the room. "Spencer brings me truffles dipped in dark chocolate and eats them with me while we watch a movie. Devin, he brings me roses, pink ones on the blush of blooming. Then there's my Byron, he brings me tickets to a gallery opening that's not his own, or tickets to see a play he'll hate and goes with me. Jamie brings me wicked things just to make me blush and because he knows that I'll call his friend and ask her about them. Nicky spends money on me foolishly because he knows that I delight in knowing he can. And Damon brings me to the cemetery on the birthdays of the two men I have loved and lost. Then he takes me to my favorite restaurant and we go home. They may not seem like special things to you, but they are from the hearts of my children. Their wives are like my daughters, every one of them have a big piece of me because they have given me a chunk of theirs."

Drew looked around the room and was astonished to see them all openly crying. He looked at Margaret and smiled. "My mother likes snowmen. Weird ones, not just the white balls stacked on top of one another. I get her one every time I see a display. I never thought about how much it meant to her." He took out his wallet and showed them a picture of her room she'd set up with them. "She sent me this last fall. She'd had the room done just for them."

Morgan took the picture last. She stared at it for a long while before handing it back to him. When she spoke Drew knew that his father was a brilliant man and planned to tell him the next time he saw him.

"She doesn't need you. Not really. No woman needs a man to dictate to them, to order them about. Nicky and I...when I found out I was pregnant with the boys, he'd arranged our wedding, where I'd live, and also who would take care of me. He never asked me, he just assumed he knew more than me and that he was going to be the boss. It wasn't until the twins were born that he realized he needed me as a part of his life and not the other way around." She wiped another tear away before she continued. "Do you love her, Drew, really love her?"

"Yes. I love her with all my heart."

She nodded. "Good, then go and get her."

CHAPTER 22

Quinn was bored. Not just bored, but out of her gourd bored. She'd already read four books and she'd decided that she hated doing crafts. Her sister didn't have a very big kitchen in her apartment so cooking wasn't that easy to do. They'd eaten out all three nights she'd been there and now she wanted a home cooked meal with all the trimmings. She was just getting ready to go to the store to get a roast when the phone rang. She groaned when she saw who it was. Pulling on her coat she didn't answer, but waited for him to leave a message.

"I know you're there, Quinn." Her heart skipped a couple of beats. If he knew then what were the chances of Drew knowing? "Drew knows too."

Fuck. She wondered if she had time to go up and pack and decided that it wouldn't be worth it. She'd just get her purse and go with the clothes on her back. Then she heard his next statement.

"Alyssa has been crying since you left. She said she wished you trusted her enough to confide in her that you were leaving. It's not good for the baby for her to be upset." Quinn sat in the chair and started crying herself. "Call her if for no other reason than to tell her you're okay. We miss you." There was a long pause. "Oh, Drew and I are in your driveway."

Quinn stared at the machine for a long moment before she got up and went to the door. Pulling back the blind she looked as there they all stood. Not just Drew and Cain, but Rose and Tommy Miller, and the lovely housekeeper Millie, Alyssa, and Jazzie. Quinn put the blind back into place and leaned her back against the door. Now what? She didn't need this right now. When the phone rang again she seriously thought about not answering it. Leaning over she looked at the caller ID and even with the thing displaying "unknown," she knew who it was.

"What?" she snarled when she snatched it up. "Do you realize that I came here to get away from your fucking ass? Leave me the fuck alone."

Silence. She peeked out the window again and saw that the only one with a phone to his ear was Thomas Miller, Drew's grandda. He waved at her.

"May I come in? I'll come alone if you'd like." He lowered his voice. "I don't know, my dear, but you might want to clean up your language before you have my great grandchild talking like that."

Quinn wanted to crawl in a hole and die. She didn't want to talk to anyone, but she hadn't thought of this kid as being anyone's but hers and Mr. Miller's.

"Come in, but alone. I don't have the energy to deal with him just now. I have a doctor's appointment to go to in two hours and I don't want to have my blood pressure up and he makes me high risk."

"Of course, my dear. My daughter Rose will be put out of joint, but I'm sure she'll understand." She knew what he was doing and let him play her anyway.

"All right, bring her too, but nobody else. I think I should be able to handle the two of you."

He didn't say anything for several seconds. "Tommy, my son, he said that he has something to say to you and then he'll come right back out. He promised."

Quinn frowned. "Mr. Miller, you do know that I'm not stupid, don't you? I mean, I can see what you're doing."

"And what is that, my dear? I'm just an old man who wants to talk to the lovely woman who is carrying his great grandchild, my future, as they say. Can you see that the next generation needs to be reassured that you are okay as well?"

Quinn looked out the blind again. He was one slick old man, she'd give him that. If she let all of them in Alyssa would be even more hurt at her, then Cain. He was her brother and this was technically not her house, but another sister of Cain's. She started to pound her head against the door frame.

"Are you always going to be this way?" His laughter made her look out the window again.

"I suppose so. You can't blame me for trying though." He laughed again. "Will you please let us in, my dear? We do mean to talk to you. I promise you with all my heart that I won't let my grandson…what did you call it, Rose? Ah yes, 'piss you the fuck off.' Quite colorful, my daughter, wouldn't you agree?"

Quinn couldn't help it, she burst out laughing. She moved the blind again and spoke to Mr. Miller, looking right at him.

"If you make me one more promise I will try my very best to try and get along with Drew while you're here."

He didn't even hesitate. "Anything. You name it and it's yours."

"You will teach my child how to be as charming as you are and that, when he wants to know, you'll tell him that I tried my very best."

He took a step away from the others before he answered. "I'm dying, child. I'm an old man who is in his later years. But I will teach our baby how to be loved; the rest is up to you and Andrew. And the babe will always know that you did your very best, my dear. You will love him and that's all that matters."

Instead of letting them in the house she opened the door and went out to them. The first thing she did was hug Mr. Miller very tightly. When he pulled back she could see tears in his eyes.

"There's my girl," he told her before he hugged her again.

They all went into house and sat down. Immediately Rose hopped up and asked to use the kitchen. She said that she cooked when she was stressed and had been itching to whip something up. Oh, and could Alyssa, Cain, Tommy and Thomas come and help? Jazzie didn't cook, but she tagged along with them.

"My family, they're not fooling anyone, are they?" Drew said when they left them alone. Quinn shook her head.

"Not really." She sat down in the big chair next to the couch. "What do you want? I thought I made my position perfectly clear on this baby."

He got down on his knees and walked across the floor toward her that way. She was so stunned that she didn't move. It wasn't until he laid his head in her lap that she realized what he'd done.

"I love you, Quinn. I will always love you. And I'm so very sorry. I was an ass like you said and a prick like…well, my family isn't happy with me either. Not that it has any bearing on how I feel about you. I just wanted…I'm screwing this up." He laid his hand over her belly. "Our child grows there. Ours. Not mine and not yours, but…he was created because you loved me long before I realized that I loved you. He is there because you wanted me."

She looked away from him. She didn't want him in her life. He was the father of her child, not anything more, and she wouldn't let him be.

"You don't have to do this. I already told you that I'd not keep you—"

His mouth covered hers. It was hot and demanding, a kiss that stole her breath and quickened her heart. Before she knew it she had her fingers in his hair and held him to her. Nothing else mattered.

She felt his hand slide beneath her ass and he pulled her forward. He was already between her legs so when she was at the edge of the seat she wrapped her legs around him and hooked her ankles at his back. She wondered fleetingly if it would always be like this between them, consuming and fast. When he cupped her breast she moaned deep in her throat.

"Please, baby, I want you." He slid his hand up her skirt and she felt her panties soak and another moan spill from her mouth. His hand seemed to be everywhere and she wondered what it would be like when he didn't have a sling on.

A noise from the kitchen had them pull apart, but not completely. They were both breathing hard and the look in his eyes was dark and hungry. She knew without a doubt that he wanted her and, fool that she was, she wanted him as well.

"We can't keep doing this. We have to figure this—" His mouth took hers again. When he pulled back she put her hand over his mouth and tried again. He whirled his tongue against her palm and made her nearly cross-eyed with need.

"Quinn, if I'm not in you very soon my family and yours is going to see a raging hard-on all night. I need you." She wanted him too and nodded. "Where? Tell me there is a room close that has a lock on the door."

"My room, the one I've been using. It's just over there." He stood up so quickly she nearly squealed. His mouth was the only thing that kept her from doing so.

Before she could say anything else he had her across the room and inside the bathroom. She giggled when he growled. He sat her on the counter and turned to lock the door.

"It'll have to do. I promise, next time, there will be a bed." Sitting down on the commode, he pulled her to the edge of the counter and looked up from between her legs.

Her heart started pounding in her chest when she realized what he was going to do.

"Drew, we can't do this. Your family is just down the hall. They'll hear us. I don't think I could bear that."

He turned around, grabbed a hand towel, and handed it to her. "Use this, but don't try and stop me. I need to taste you. Now."

She looked at the hand towel and felt his finger slide into her. She nearly yelled, but stuffed the towel in her mouth and closed her eyes. Now she understood what he wanted when he handed her the thing.

"You're so wet for me. Christ, I can smell your heat. I want to eat you. I'm going to lick you until you can't stand it then I'm going to pick you up, bend you over this counter, and fuck you hard. Is that what you want?" Quinn nodded. "Good. But you have to be quiet, love."

His fingers were replaced with his mouth. She did scream then and the only thing keeping the entire neighborhood from hearing was the navy blue towel in her hand. But he didn't let her come.

Each time she was ready to explode he'd move and she'd calm down only to have him start anew somewhere else. Her body ached for a release from his torment. She was sobbing by the time he stood up and unsnapped his pants.

"Stand up. I'm going to fuck you now. I'm so needy I hurt." She watched as he freed his cock. He was so hard that it looked painful. When she reached out and wrapped her hand around him she couldn't believe how incredibly hot he was. When she began sliding her hand up and down him he wrapped his hand around hers and slowed her down.

"I'm so close right now, baby, that for as good as this feels, you keep it up and I'm going to come all over you." Finally he pulled her hand back and put it on the counter. "Fuck, I want you."

Quinn scrambled off the counter and turned around. He lifted her skirt up off her ass and pulled her panties down to her knees. She was so wet she could feel it trickle down her thighs. She spread her legs wide and let him see how wet she was and nearly came when he ran is tongue along the seam of her ass.

She moaned out his name as he stood behind her. Quinn looked at him in the mirror. Hunger was there, but something else, something more. She recognized it as soon as he kissed her shoulder. He really did love her.

"I'm going to take you, Quinn. And for as much as I want it to be slow and easy, I'm not sure I can do that with you. When you're wrapped around me, holding me tight inside of you, I can't seem to think of anything else but marking you as mine." He slid inside of her and moaned. "Christ, you're so tight, so wet for me. When I taste your cream on my tongue and my mouth it's all I can do not to pound into you."

He moved back and slowly slid into her again. He moved until she thought she was going to scream. When she moved back against him he nipped at her shoulder and growled.

"Drew, please. I need to come, please?" She tried moving back against him again, hoping he'd fuck her now. But he bit her harder and stayed her by wrapping his hand around her waist.

He looked at her in the mirror again. His eyes were dark and hooded. She could see the strain he was under, sweat beaded on his forehead and his chin. She couldn't look away if her life depended on it.

"Marry me, Quinn. Marry me so that I can do this with you every day. I want to wake up next to you every morning and hold you." He slid inside of her again, harder this time, and slid his hand down to her pussy and pinched her clit. "I love you. I want you to be my wife. Please?"

The next time he slid in and out of her he hit her spot, the one that nearly sent her over the edge. He must have known it because the next time he moved he pulled at her clit and rocked harder. When he whispered against her shoulder to "come" her body came apart. And she remembered the towel when she screamed out her approval.

CHAPTER 23

Drew tried hard not to smile, but it was difficult. Every time someone looked at Quinn she would flare up again. When she'd come like she had and screamed out her "yes" at the top of her lungs his family had come running thinking she'd agreed to his proposal.

Alyssa kept winking at him and Cain just glared. Drew was having a great time. And he felt more relaxed than he had in months. He reached over and took her hand again. He loved her so much that he didn't mind that she smacked him every time he kissed her wrist.

"So," his father started. "You two work out your differences?" Alyssa laughed and Cain blustered.

"No, we have not, thank you very much. I'm still not marrying him. I don't know why you all have a problem with that. It's not as though people aren't having babies all the time without marrying anyone. Oh shi…crap, I forgot my appointment. They'll charge me for it even though I didn't make it."

"I'm okay with you not marrying me. I just want to make sure you are going to let me into our baby's life." He was taking a big gamble, but one he hoped would pay off. "Would you live with me, Quinn?"

"Now just a damned minute. You'll marry my sister or else. I mean it—"

"Hush, Cain." Alyssa cut him off. "Are you okay with that, Quinn? Living with Drew?"

"I guess so. I mean…why are you all of a sudden okay with me not marrying you? I thought you were all set to make me." Quinn looked at him and he shrugged. "You don't want to marry me?"

"Sure I do. I love you very much. But I want you to be happy. That and the fact that I want to see our child grow up that way too has changed my mind." He turned to her and took her hand. "I love you, Quinn. I've been an ass and a prick. But I want to change. I want to be with you more than anything in this world. So if you say you don't want to get married, then I'll just have to live with that."

She looked at him oddly. He had to turn away or beg her to marry him. He looked over at his grandda, who winked. Yeah, he would get it. So would his dad, but he was afraid to look at him.

"You drive me nuts, do you know that?" When she stood up, so did all the men at the table. With a glare around the room, they all sat except for him.

"Honey, I—"

"Don't you 'honey' me, you moron. What's wrong with being married to me? Huh? Are you thinking I'm good enough to screw but not be your wife?"

He did look at his dad now. He was on dangerous territory here and he was in a mine field of bombs. Panicky, he reached for whatever he could. He dropped to one knee and pulled out the blue box. "Then say yes. Tell me right now that you'll be my wife and we'll get married in the morning."

The look she gave him was priceless, and scary too. With trembling hands she took the box from him and opened it. He didn't say anything as she opened it and closed her eyes. He didn't know if she liked it or not until she dropped down on her knees before him and kissed him.

"You really want to marry me? You bought the ring and...it's so beautiful." She kissed him again as he took the box from her. "Oh Drew, it's so beautiful."

"It's not new. I'm sorry, if you want new I can...it's my grandma's. I've had it for a long time. My grand...she gave it to me when I turned eighteen. I've never considered giving it to anyone else before." He slipped it on her finger. "I knew it would fit."

It did look lovely on her hand. It was a three-carat yellow diamond with small half-carat rubies and sapphires around it. The white gold band had an inscription on the inside that said simply, "I will love you for all my days." He couldn't have said it better himself. When she looked up at him from their kneeling position on the floor he smiled.

"I love you, Quinn. So very much."

"I love you too."

The family rushed them then. To be honest, Drew had completely forgotten they were there after he dropped to his knee. His grandda hugged him and he kissed Quinn. When his mom and dad crowded in, Cain picked up his sister and held her up for a second then put her down again. Then he gave him another hug.

Drew was sure that he'd have broken ribs by morning, but didn't really mind all that much. He had a beautiful wife-to-be and a baby on the way. Holding her hand they ate dinner as the family made plans for the wedding. Drew watched as his grandda stood up and set his knife to his glass.

"I have something I'd like to say, if you please." The room got silent and he nodded at Millie just inside the doorway. As she disappeared Grandda turned back to them. "When my Abida passed on many years ago she made me promise that I would give this to you when you found a woman you wanted to spend your life with. She told me that you would find a woman who would never bow to your demands and she would be the center of your universe because you'd love deeply and wholly." He lifted his glass to Quinn. "It seems she was right on both predictions."

Quinn got up and hugged him to her. There were tears around the table as he told her he loved her as much as he did Drew and that he would be honored if she called him Grandda. When Millie brought a large box in and set it on the floor beside them his grandda cleared a few plates out to the way to set the box on the table.

"I think it will fit." He helped Quinn open the box. "It was ours. She wore this, as did Drew's mother when she married my son. I hope even if you change the ring that you would honor my wife and wear it for her."

Quinn was sobbing now as she moved tissue paper and wrapping out of the way. When she gasped Drew stood to go over next to her. Inside the box was his grandma's wedding gown and veil. As she fingered the white lace and satin buttons Quinn smiled.

"I don't want another ring. This one is perfect. And the dress...I don't know what to say. It's the most...there are no words to describe how much I'm...how touched I am that you want me to wear this." She turned to him. "You sure about this? I don't want to get my hopes dashed about becoming a part of this family only to have you change your mind."

"I've never been surer of anything in my life. I love you."

~~~

Quinn was nervous. She wasn't sure if Drew would come to her bed tonight or not. Lilliane had given him sheets and blankets and told him the couch was comfortable then went off to bed. Cain and Alyssa had gone to one of their hotels, taking Drew's family with them. She got up and made sure the door was unlocked again. She was just touching the knob to do so when it turned.

Snatching back her hand, she watched as it turned slowly then opened. When Drew slipped in she nearly screamed when he pulled her against him and kissed her.

"Hummm, what a way to be greeted. I think I'll get to liking this." Then he kissed her again.

She felt the bed hit the back of her legs before she even realized that they had moved. When he reached down and took her silk-covered nipple into his mouth Quinn couldn't help but moan.

"Christ, I love making you do that. That sound goes straight to my cock." He pulled her gown up and over her head and dropped it on the floor behind him. "You are so sexy."

The bra and panty set had been a gift from Sin when she'd been on leave last month. It was a dark blue and black with very little to each piece other than scraps of lace and some elastic. Drew ran his thumbs up and under the cups of the bra as he took her breast into his mouth again.

Reaching down, she cupped his cock in her hand and with more concentration than she thought she had, she rubbed him up and down until he stepped back.

"Lay down. I want to feast on you."

She started to do that when she suddenly wanted him. "No, you lay down. I want to feast on you for a change." When he started to take off his pants first she dropped to her knees and pushed his hands away. "Let me. I want to taste your cock first."

Taking a man's belt off from beneath him wasn't as easy as it looked. She had to reach up and try to figure out how it fit together while his cock was right there. To distract him from seeing how clumsy she was at it she rubbed her cheek along the length of him. He seemed to enjoy that very much. When she got the belt open she put her hands on the back of his pants and cupped his ass. She loved watching his face every time she touched him.

"Quinn, if you keep that up I'm going to come in my pants like a kid. Free me so that you can take me into your mouth so I can fuck it." Her pussy gushed cream at his words. "That's it, baby."

She nearly had his zipper down when she could see the dark hair nestled there. Running her tongue up and over the exposed area, she nearly came when he groaned.

Getting his pants down became a challenge because she kept getting distracted by the warm flesh she'd reveal. When his cock was finally free she licked him from base to tip in a long, wet lick. His hand in her hair tightened painfully, but she didn't stop. Quinn was determined to enjoy herself.

Working her way from the root of his cock, she nipped at him. Every time she would give his tiny wound an open-mouthed kiss before moving up to start again. When she got to the bulbous head she swirled her tongue around it before taking it into her mouth and swallowing. Drew groaned out her name in a long single syllable word.

She wrapped her hand around his cock and, using her own saliva, she worked her hand up and down as she tasted him. His cock was thick and long and she could barely breathe around him when he was inside of her mouth. When he tightened his grip in her hair and pulled her back she dug her nails into his ass and looked up at him.

"I want to be inside of you…I'm not…Christ, you're killing me, baby. Let me fuck your pussy, please." His voice was rough, his tone pleading, but she didn't want to stop.

"Come in my mouth, Drew. I want you to shoot your cum down my throat so I can taste you." She wrapped her mouth around him again and watched his face.

He didn't take his eyes from hers as he began rocking in her mouth. His hand at the back of her head held her steady as his thrusts got harder and faster. When she felt the first hot stream hit her tongue, she took him deeper into her, felt him slide down her throat. He didn't stop. He fucked her mouth hard and long. When he pulled her back this time she let him go. Suddenly she was up and his mouth was ravaging hers.

"Quinn," he said hoarsely against her mouth. "Lay down. It's my turn."

When she scrambled onto the bed and lay on her back he told her to turn around and get on her knees. She loved it when he took her from behind and hurried to do what he wanted. When his hand slapped hard at her ass she sat up and turned around, ready to blast him with her temper.

"No, turn around." His voice was hard. "I'm going to beat this beautiful ass of yours until it's hot then I'm going to fuck you hard. You'll learn to obey me in the bedroom, Quinn, or you'll get this every night."

Her pussy clenched at the thought of him spanking her. She turned around and before she could settle back onto the bed he slapped her again.

"When I tell you to stop sucking my dick so I can fuck you"—slap, then another— "you'll do it." Two more and her ass hurt.

When he slid his hand between her legs and pinched her clit she rolled into his hand. She could feel her juices flood his hand.

"You're so wet. I'm going to enjoy this so much. Have you ever had your ass fucked, baby?"

"Carl…he did it. But I didn't…he hurt me." She hated bringing him to her bed, but didn't want to start screaming if Drew tried like she had with Carl.

"Remind me to kill that bastard. I'm not going to hurt you, baby. I'm going to go slow and easy. If I hurt you, I swear to you I'll stop. All right?"

She was terrified. She didn't want to disappoint him, but she had been hit so many times during sex that she almost said no. But this was Drew and he loved her. Before she could change her mind she nodded.

"Good girl. Tell me when you want me to stop." He moved his fingers to her pussy again and she felt his cock nudge at her entrance. "I'm going to use your cream to get you ready for me. Christ, you are so fucking wet. I could fill my mouth with you. And you taste so delicious, hot and spicy. I love tasting you after I come inside of you."

She relaxed by degrees. When she started to rock into his hand he bit her shoulder. When he touched her tight hole she tensed up again.

"No, don't. I'm not…I'm only going to use my thumb. Feel it?" His thumb pressed against her rings and she was soon arching up to get more of him. When he broke, though, and was inside of her she felt a slight pain, but nothing like she had before.

"Are you all right?" She nodded. "You're so tight back here. I'm going to enjoy fucking you. I want to come deep in your ass and make you scream. I'm going to buy you a toy when we get home. One that I can vibrate your clit with while a fuck this ass of mine. You'll come so hard you will pass out from it."

She wanted to come now. Her ass no longer hurt, but felt good. Her pussy was fluttering with each stroke of his fingers against her. When he moved away from her pussy she whimpered and he chuckled.

"I'm going to stretch you now and need more of your cream. I won't let you suffer. Not too much anyway."

When he moved back to her clit and pinched her she came. Not hard, but enough to flood his hand and make her want more.

"That's it, baby. I'll let you come now, but when we get home you'll ask me. I want you to know that I'm the master in here. All right?"

"You...you are into games?" Her body was beginning to build up to another climax, quicker this time. "You want to tie me up and whip me?"

He stopped what he was doing and answered her. "Yes. I'm into games. Nothing too hard core, but I do enjoy them. Are you all right with that?

Before she could answer she felt her ass pinch as he moved inside her. She didn't hurt, not really, but found she wanted him to move, to take her.

"I've...I've never played before. But if you teach me, I think I'd like it. Especially if it feels this good." She arched back against his fingers as they stretched her. "Please, Drew, more."

His laugher sent a shiver down her spine. When he leaned over and bit her again, this time harder, she came again. Another quick fighting of her body and a sudden release.

Soon they had a rhythm. He would gather more of her cream and then work her ass until she was comfortable, begging him for more. His bites got harder, but not painful, his mouth hotter, but not mean. When he leaned over her back and nipped her shoulder again she could feel his hot, heavy breath on her neck.

"I'm going to enter you now. I'm can't wait much…I won't hurt you, but your ass is driving me crazy and I need to be inside you." She nodded.

When his finger pulled out of her she whimpered again. She found that she loved that full feeling and wanted more of it. His cock at her pussy stroking along her folds made her reach between her legs and try to guild him inside.

"No, baby. I'm getting my cock wet so I can slide easier. Christ, your pussy is hot and I'm going to have to suck you off again and again just to satisfy my craving for you."

When his cock was back at her ass she tensed up. His hand coming across her ass had her moan. "Good girl. Now I'm going to go slow, but I won't be able to if you move like that again. Take a deep breath and, when I tell you, release it slowly but don't tense up or it will hurt."

Nodding again, she took a deep breath and when he told her, she slowly let it out. His cock pushed hard against her ass and she felt a sudden pop and he was in.

The pain was overwhelming and she nearly screamed for him to stop. But he didn't move, didn't so much as lean on her.

"I'm inside of you Quinn and you cannot believe how incredible it feels to have you pulsing around my dick. If I don't move soon I'm going to come just here and you won't be able to feel me moving inside of you."

He moved slightly, his cock going deeper into her until she tensed, then he moved back. Over and over he moved this way, deeper each time. When she felt his groin against her pussy she knew that he was all the way inside. His harsh breathing made her realize how much this was hurting him too.

"Drew, please, I want you to come inside of me. Fuck me, please. I want to feel you fuck me this way." Arching back against him she felt the first bit of pleasure. As he started moving slowly she bowed her back and spread her legs wider, taking him deeper.

When he reached between her legs and entered her pussy she came apart. The small climaxes she'd had were only a teaser. This one ripped through her body and she saw stars. Burying her head in her pillow she screamed over and over as he fucked her. When he stiffened over her she felt his cum splash deep inside of her and it brought her again. He was moving faster now, both his cock and his fingers. When she came a third time he sat up, grabbed her hip, and pistoned deep.

Quinn collapsed on the bed when he dropped onto her. She couldn't move, wasn't sure if she would be able to ever again. Drew rolled to his side and when he was on his back, he pulled her to his chest where she promptly fell asleep.

CHAPTER 24

The funeral for Alyssa's mother was held at the local funeral home. Thousands turned out on the cold, blustery morning. There were whispers about how Shannon had died, who had killed her. There was always talk when a woman as beautiful as her mother was killed. Alyssa and Cain sat in the front rows along with four of his five sisters. Sydney couldn't be reached in time to make it home. Right behind them sat the entire Miller family. Nathan couldn't attend, of course. He was "drying out." There was a lot of talk about Robert, but no one really cared, especially not Alyssa.

The graveside services for her brother had been held the day before. There hadn't been anything in the paper, just as Alyssa had wanted, and there had been no one there save the funeral director and Drew. He wasn't buried in the family plot either, and there would be no marker until after the trial. Even though he was dead there would still be a murder trial brought against him. Alyssa needed this and was glad when it was over for the closure. She had just one more thing to do.

The DVDs that Quinn had told the police about had showed that Samuel had been aware of his nephew's actions that day. It had also, on other recordings, showed him as a perverted man. He had brought small boys into the house and had raped them. He didn't have a gambling problem as they had thought, but used his money to pay off families of his victims. He, too, was standing trial, though for now it was very quiet.

The week after the funeral Alyssa left work early and went to pay a visit. No one knew where she was going except the bodyguard with her and her husband. He didn't want her to go, but she had been asked and she would do this one thing for him.

~~~

Nathan paced his room again. He was nervous. What if she didn't come? What if she changed her mind? He didn't know if he'd be happy about that or sad. He sat down again only to hop back up and begin pacing again.

"If you wear a hole in the floor you won't get your deposit back. And from what I understand, it's a hefty one."

Nathan looked over at the man who had been his nurse for the past thirteen months. "Did she call and say she wasn't coming? I knew this was a bad idea. Not only have I set myself up for this, but she will know I'm a loser."

Brady came in the room and sat on the chair. "No, she didn't call. She said she'd be here and she will. And if I hear you call yourself a loser again I'll take away your pudding at dinner and give it to old lady Bird and tell her you're sweet on her."

Nathan smiled. Mrs. Bird had been in this place and out again twice since he'd been here. He was not going to be a repeater, he'd decided. He'd been told that if a person could make it an entire year without an episode it got easier each time.

"What if she doesn't come? What if...what if she laughs at me and tells me to fuck off?" Nathan sat down. "I don't think I can do this."

"You're going to be fine. Take a deep breath and let it out slowly. She's coming. I wasn't going to tell you this, but she called this morning and asked for directions. She said she had a negative sense of direction and wanted to make sure she didn't get lost." Nathan looked at the man in the chair as he laughed. "Sound like someone else you know?"

Nathan could get lost in his own room. Not really that bad, but he couldn't find his way around the grounds without a map to guide him. He did do better once he got some landmarks memorized, but somewhere new, he'd never make it.

He started to pace again when his phone rang. It always startled him because he hadn't had one until recently. He was beginning to get all sorts of things now that he could go for days without the shakes and he wasn't talking about killing himself any more. He still got depressed, majorly, but he was getting better at handling it.

With shaky hands he picked it up and said hello.

"Mr. Howard, you have a visitor at the front desk. Would you like for us to bring her to you or do you want to come and get her?"

"I'll come and get her. Thank you, Marsha. I appreciate it." He hung up the phone and turned to Brady. "She's here. I'm going to be sick."

"No, you're not. Go and see your sister. You'll be fine, and Nathan? Don't forget why you asked her here."

Nathan nodded as he left the room. He had to ask her to forgive him. It was part of his process. She didn't have to forgive him, but he had to ask all the same. When he got to the desk there was a woman there with Marsha, and a man. Nathan didn't know either of them. He walked forward, taking deep breaths as he went, and plastered on what he hoped passed as a smile.

"Hi. I'm Nathan Howard." He closed his eyes at his blunder. "I'm sorry. I've been…I've been drunk and high for so long, I don't…this was a mistake. I'm sorry. I thank you for coming." When he turned to leave, run as a matter of fact, she laughed. A soft sound that brought up all sorts of disjointed memories. He stopped and turned back to her. "You used to do that. Laugh when you were nervous. I remember that. I don't remember much, but that I do."

She smiled again. "I'm Alyssa Waite. This is one of my bodyguards, Daniel Louise. I don't remember much about you either."

Nathan looked at the bodyguard and nodded. Turning back to his sister he whispered, "I'd never hurt you. I don't know if I did in the past, but I would never harm you. Ever."

She glanced back at Daniel and he stepped away. Not far, but he did give them privacy. "He's not because of you. I'm…there are people who would harm me and my husband is overprotective. Overbearing as well, but mostly overprotective of me. Can we sit down?"

Nathan led her to the sitting area for visitors. He waited until she sat then he sat across from her. He was suddenly nervous again. The beautiful woman before him wasn't what he expected.

"I was thinking of you as a child. I know that's stupid, but I didn't picture you as a woman." When she laughed he blushed. "I'm sorry, that didn't come out right. I'm not very good…I need to tell you I'm sorry."

"For what? And you never hurt me. Not physically anyway. You and I didn't run in the same crowds so there was nothing there. You have nothing to be sorry for, Nathan."

He looked around the room. He wanted to do this right. She was being really nice to him and he didn't know how to handle it. His family just wasn't nice.

"I know about…I know about Shannon. And Robert. They said that he killed her, is that true?" She nodded. "She wasn't a nice person. I mean…they said that you can't blame someone else for your problems, but she is the reason I'm a drunk and an addict. She gave me my first drink when I was ten."

"That sounds like her. She would have wanted to control you with it. I'm the one who should be sorry. She…Dad told me once that she was the root of all evil. I didn't know what he meant until that night we met in the restaurant."

Nathan didn't remember that night, or for that matter much after he'd turned twelve. But he only nodded.

"Uncle Samuel...he's not nice either. He...he's evil. You need to stay away from him or have your bodyguard close. Don't let him touch you." He took a deep breath when the guard stepped toward them. He hadn't realized his voice had risen.

She lifted her hand and Daniel didn't move any closer, but he didn't stop staring hard at him. Alyssa leaned forward then, took his chin and pulled his gaze from the man behind her.

"Nathan, did Uncle Samuel molest you? Did he hurt you?" Nathan tried to look away, but she gripped him harder. "Answer me please?"

"I was seven. He said that...he told me that he was going to show me something fun. It wasn't fun. It was...it was horrible. After a while Shannon would bring me to him when I refused to go. I hated her for that, and him. I will never be able to..."

She got up and sat next to him on the couch and pulled him into her arms. Nathan didn't know what to do at first. It was his first hug in more years than he could remember. A hug given for comfort, not because he needed to be held down. He wrapped his arms around her and started crying. Soon it was sobs. He thought for a second he should be ashamed, but all he could think about was that she was holding him and not condemning him.

After a bit he just let her hold him, his tears dried now. When he sat up he noticed that Daniel and his nurse were gone and that there was no one else in the lobby. He smiled at her.

"They were staring at us. I thought it best if we had some private time." He sat back on the couch and smiled at her. "You've had it rough, haven't you?"

He looked around the lobby again. He'd been here for over a year now and his time was almost up. He'd be out in another ten days as a matter of fact. Nathan didn't know what he was going to do, where he was going, but he was going to make something of himself.

"It's not been so bad, not here anyway. I know you've been paying for this and you have no idea how much I appreciate it. This place...it's been where I began my life. I've been making plans. I've taken some college classes in the past six months. Nothing too stressful at first, but I'm getting better. I've been working on a degree in business management. I want to help people that have been...you don't care. I just wanted to tell—"

"Don't do that, Nathan. I do care. I didn't think I would, but I do. Tell me about your classes. I want to hear." She leaned back against the back of the couch and that's when he noticed her belly.

"You're pregnant. That's...you said you were married, but it didn't register. A baby, my baby sister is going to have a baby." He started to reach out and put his hand on her, but pulled it back.

"It's all right, you can feel him." She took his hand and put it on her belly. "He doesn't move yet...well, not so you can feel him. But I can feel it, a quick kind of swirl in my belly. It's so cool."

Nathan didn't feel anything but her tiny belly. It was hard and soft at the same time. He couldn't believe she was old enough to be pregnant. He smiled when she grinned at him.

"Your husband, he's a good man? I don't know him...do I?"

"No, his name is Cain Waite. You'll like him, he's a doctor. He has these sisters, five of them. They are incredible. I can't wait for you to meet them. Nathan?"

He pulled his hand away and turned from her. "I didn't ask...you don't have to say that, Alyssa. I'm just so happy that you came here to see me. And to let me tell you how sorry I am."

He heard her shift on the couch. "Nathan, look at me. I mean it, look at me."

He turned slowly. He wasn't sure what he expected, but the tears in her eyes weren't it. He nearly turned away, but she grabbed his chin again.

"You're going to be bruised if you don't stop not listening to me." Her smile was wobbly. "I didn't come here expecting anything other than to visit a man from my past. What I got was something more. When you leave here in two weeks you'll be coming home to my house for a few days. The man I talked to earlier said you needed to go to a halfway house for a month then you'd be free to do as you please so long as you got a job and didn't have any setbacks. Is that right?"

"Yes. I have to get a job or go to school full time. But I'm not expecting you to—"

"Hush, I'm not finished. You'll have a job if you want it. And if you want to go to school I'll help you with that as well. You're all the family I have and we have to work together. I want you to be in my life. If you don't want to be in mine…well, tough shit. You're stuck with me."

Nathan laughed. "Does that work on your husband?"

"No, not nearly as much as I'd like for it to. But it works wonders in the board room and with the city council. I mean it. You'll come home with me. I live in the old house, but you know there is plenty of—"

"I can't live there." He felt the panic rise. "I'll work or go to school with…please don't make me live there."

She took his hands in hers and held him until it passed. He knew she was saying something, but he hadn't understood until he felt calmer.

"I'm sorry. I didn't think. There's a house on the other property. It's not far from where we live, you'll stay there. No one is there anymore. Jazzie lives in the big house, but the cottage will be perfect for you."

"Why are you being so nice to me, Alyssa? I mean, you don't owe me anything. Right after you came back an attorney came and brought me the paperwork…I know that I've spent a great deal of your money…why?"

She looked around the room now and was quiet for a long time. Nathan let her be. He enjoyed the quiet too.

"Let me do this for you. I don't know…I'm not sure why I want to do this yet myself, but I want to do this for you, for us." She turned back to him. "Will you let me?"

Nathan nodded. He didn't know either and he found he didn't want to disappoint her.

CHAPTER 25

The morning of the wedding dawned bright and sunny. Quinn had fought him all the way on a big wedding, but he was sure that someday, hopefully soon, she'd appreciate it. He looked over at his best man and smiled.

"Here, let me, Grandda. You're making it worse. How did you ever wear a suit and tie everyday to work?"

He huffed. "Your grandma did it for me. Said it made her feel useful. Made me feel stupid. Why do we have to get dressed like damned penguins for anyway? Just to say I do."

Drew laughed. "Because Quinn is going to have the wedding of my dreams. And because you want to see her dressed up in Grandma's wedding dress."

Grandda put his hands over his to still him. Drew looked up into his face. There was sadness there and Drew was suddenly sorry for it.

"Grandda, I didn't mean—"

"She would have loved your Quinny. Loved her smart mouth and the way she keeps you in line. Couldn't have picked a better girl for you even if I'd tried. Nope, you don't look at this old man like I'm sad. I couldn't be happier. But I miss my Adie. Miss her more and more as the years go on."

Drew hugged his grandda tight. The man was his best friend in the entire world and he was lucky to have him. When Drew felt a hand on his back he knew without looking it was his dad. His comforting hand could do wonders to him.

"If the love fest is about over, you think maybe we can get this show on the road? I got a wife I want to molest," Cain said with a slap on the older man's back.

"Young man, there are more things in life than sex, you know?" Grandda said as he walked toward the door.

"Yeah, I know that. But I doubt there is anything quite as enjoyable. Especially when you have a beautiful wife like I do." Cain laughed when Grandda huffed.

As the other men walked out the door Drew's dad and grandda stayed a little behind. He smiled at them when they looked so serious. He knew this was coming, had known for three days.

"Your mother wants to know if you need anything…advice." His dad flushed. "I mean on…shit, this is stupid. Your wife is pregnant. I'm pretty sure he knows what he's about."

Grandda laughed. "Yes, but we needed to see you get all embarrassed, son. It's what I live for. I put her up to it and Rose loves me a good deal more than you. I hear you pissed her off something fierce this morning."

Drew looked at his dad. "You ticked off Mom? What did you do?" His dad flushed harder. "Or do I want to know?"

"No, you don't. Now I agree with Cain, it's time to get moving." His dad stalked to the door before he stopped and looked back. "Stay out of this, Dad, I mean it. You tell him and I'll make your life a living hell for a week."

As he went out the door Drew turned to his grandda. "I haven't a clue what he did. I only hinted to him that she'd told me. But it is funny to see him all flustered like that, huh?"

Drew threw his arm around his grandda and laughed. He loved this old man and would never forget him. As they made their way to the vestibule Drew turned to him. "I love you. I'm so glad you agreed to stand up with me. I want to give you your wedding gift now. Quinn said you'd like it." He reached into his pocket, pulled out a sheet of paper, and handed it to him. "Dane Grant came by a couple of day ago and told us. We wanted you to be the first to know."

He looked confused and handed it back to Drew. "I don't know what this is."

Drew looked at the note and smiled. It said 1g-2b. "It's the baby. Well, babies. One girl and two boys. We're having triples. The girl will be Abida Rose Miller and the boys will be Thomas Andrew Miller the sixth and James Allen Mil—" He was being hugged so tightly he was sure he'd have to have Cain check him out for broken ribs.

"Babies. I'm going to be a first time great grandda three times. Three of them. And Abida? You're going to name your daughter Abida. Oh Drew." This hug was just a powerful, but Drew had been prepared.

His dad came back and cleared his throat. "It's time, son. Let's go and get me a daughter."

The bridesmaids were all dressed in summer colors. They were her sisters, all but Sydney. But Drew barely registered them; he was waiting on his bride. When the music sounded to announce her coming he looked up and saw Cain first. The man simply made a tux look good. But once Drew saw Quinn, his Quinn, nothing else mattered.

His grandma's dress fit just like his grandda had said it would. The ivory taffeta gown had no straps, but the full bodice held her up and kept her fuller figure from spilling out. The wide skirt didn't hide her swollen belly, but seemed to announce it to everyone who saw her that she was pregnant. The beaded work and the fine lace looked so feminine on her that he wanted to drop to his knees and beg her to love him for all time. The veil, a long trail of lace, covered her face from her head to the bottom of her chin. Drew wanted to peel it away and taste her again.

Drew grinned when he thought about the things she had on under the dress...or what she didn't have on, and his cock twitched. Looking at her now he could see her slight blush and knew she was thinking the same thing. Drew couldn't wait to get her alone.

When she came to the front to stand before him, and before the minister could ask who gave this woman, his grandda moved up behind him and said his name. He only had to look to see that the man needed Quinn, and needed a hug.

Drew nodded once and moved to the side as his grandda moved in front of Quinn and pulled her into his arms. The entire church could hear him crying and talking to her. Quinn held him to her and cried right along with him. Drew was wiping a tear from his own eyes when he looked out at the friends and family that had come to see them married. There wasn't a dry eye in the house. When Drew's parents got up and embraced Quinn and Grandda, Drew's father pulled him close and included him. When they seemed to have things under control his grandda turned to the congregation and smiled.

"I want to say I'm not the least bit sorry for this. A man goes his entire life hoping for…hoping that his children will find love and happiness. Then when he gets blessed like I have been, he begins to hope for the same for his grandchildren. Today I welcome my newest addition to my family. Quinn Susan Waite Miller. And I have to tell you…it just doesn't get any better than this." With a final kiss to his daughter-in-law and his soon to be granddaughter his grandda moves back to Drew's right. "Well, let's get this party started, shall we?"

Drew burst out laughing and with both their families standing next to them, Quinn Susan Waite became Quinn Miller.

ABOUT THE AUTHOR

Hello! My name is Kathi Barton and I'm an author. I have been married to my very best friend Sonny for at times seems several lifetimes – in a good way, honey. And together we have three wonderful children and then the ones we brought into the world - Paul and Dale Barton, Jason and Wendy Barton and Danielle and Ben Conklin. They have given us seven of the greatest treasures on Earth. They don't live at home seven days a week! No, seriously, seven grandchildren – Gavin, Spring, Ben, Trinity, Sarah, Kelly and Kian.